RATTENBURY

A novel based on the memoirs of a
West Country Smuggler

Mary Upton

Tradewind Publications

© Mary Upton 2006
ISBN 978-0-9555825-0-9

First published in the UK by
TRADEWIND PUBLICATIONS
Clapps Lane,
Beer,
Devon
EX12 3HQ

This novel is a work of fiction. Although names and characters do belong to actual persons, now dead, any resemblance to living persons is entirely coincidental.

Printed in Great Britain by:
SRP Ltd.
25 Bittern Rd., Sowton Industrial Estate,
Exeter
Devon

Mary Upton was born in the Forest of Dean in 1942. She attended Bells Grammar School in Coleford, Gloucestershire and later qualified as a Mental Health Social Worker and Counsellor. Since retiring she has travelled extensively in the mountain regions of India and Nepal and more recently has spent four months driving through Europe in a camper van. She lives in the village of Beer and spends her time writing, gardening and riding her bike half way up hills.

ACKNOWLEDGEMENTS

I would like to thank my husband for his kindness and his heroic reserves of patience during the construction of this book. In addition, I received constant encouragement and advice from Rowland Molony, poet and writer, who helped me hold on to the belief that my scribbling would eventually emerge as something recognisable.

Thanks to Felicity, Deborah and Martin for their editing and proof reading expertise. A big thank you to my brother Harold, Kathy, Elizabeth, Marilyn, Pat, Lynne, Ken Ward and my sons Nicholas and Mark. They all patiently read through the much altered manuscript while giving me constructive and humorous feedback. Merci to Annette and Graham for enhancing the French connection.

Mike Green has been generous with information and the loan of reference books. Colin Westlake, Barry Hoare and Eddie Burrows have all given me the benefit of their sailing and seafaring knowledge. Many thanks to Nicola Burley (Heritage Vision) for her advice on cob and stone cottages. And finally, a big thank you to the unnamed people of Beer who have provided me with information in so many areas.

AUTHOR'S NOTE

Jack Rattenbury was born in Beer in 1778 and lived in the village until his death in 1844. The coastal villages of East Devon, at that time, were remote from major thoroughfares. But in 1794, the village was visited by the Reverend John Swete, who was touring Devon with two female companions. His words can aptly be used to describe the village today:

The scenery around this place is bold and romantic, the cliffs in particular hovering high. Whilst the fishing boats passing from or entering the cove, their sails arresting a beam of light, whilst scudding beneath the shaded rock, was productive of one of the most pleasing effects that a water view can afford.

Travels in Georgian Devon: The Illustrated Journals of the Reverend John Swete, 1789-1800

Jack was fifteen years of age at the outbreak of the war with France in 1793. The French Emperor, Napoleon Bonaparte, dominated Western Europe and the fear of invasion by the French was a constant preoccupation.

During the earlier years of the war England possessed enormous wealth and was sole mistress of the seas, but distribution of this wealth was partial. It remained in the hands of the landowners, farmers, merchants and manufacturers. The labouring classes experienced terrible poverty, with the inevitable result: an increase in crime. Several events contributed to this situation:

- A huge increase in the population – from ten to fifteen million over a period of fifteen years.

- The introduction of machinery, which brought ruin to a number of small trades, traditionally carried on in the home.

- A series of poor harvests and an interruption to the import of wheat from America, caused by the war with France. These events resulted in the cost of wheat rising to famine-inducing prices.

This unhappy situation applied to East Devon as much as anywhere else in the country and it was inevitable that men and women would use whatever opportunities became available to them to provide for their families, and avoid taking charity. During this period the chief economic activities in Beer were fishing, farming, quarrying and lace-making. But the village was a secret tucked-away place, which made it ideal for the lucrative and respected profession of smuggling. Jack Rattenbury and his associates used the terrain and exploited the inefficient Excise Service to good effect. Communication between the service and the army reinforcements (Dragoons) was poor and this enabled Jack to avoid capture on many occasions. In fact he was notorious for his exploits and rejoiced in the nickname 'Rob Roy of the West'.

In the early days, smuggling took the form of illegal exportation rather than importation, and was directly concerned with the wool trade. The export of raw wool was prohibited by the Government in an attempt to protect the home weaving industry. The original wool smugglers were known as 'Owlers' because they worked by night.

Import smuggling (as we now know it) grew up when customs dues were first introduced. Duties were levied on tobacco, tea, brandy, rum, silks, muslin, handkerchiefs and even salt. It was once estimated that, if all the goods smuggled into Falmouth alone in the course of one year had been taxed, the money collected would have been more than twice the land tax for the whole kingdom.

The eighteenth-century economist Adam Smith defined a smuggler (or Fair Trader, as they preferred to call themselves) as:

'A person who, though no doubt highly blameable for violating the laws of his country, is frequently incapable of violating those of natural justice and who would have been in every respect an excellent citizen had not the laws of his country made that a crime which Nature never meant to be so.'

This attitude was widespread in the poverty-stricken inhabitants of Beer and they held the Government's customs duties in the greatest contempt.

Today, you have only to sit on the beach for a while and observe the way both men and boys handle and sail their boats, to witness the skill which helped their forefathers survive those desperate times.

Rattenbury is based on Jack's own book, *Memoirs of a Smuggler,* and extensive research of life in those times. In order to bring Jack and his family to life I have needed to exercise some fictional licence, as I trust the reader will appreciate.

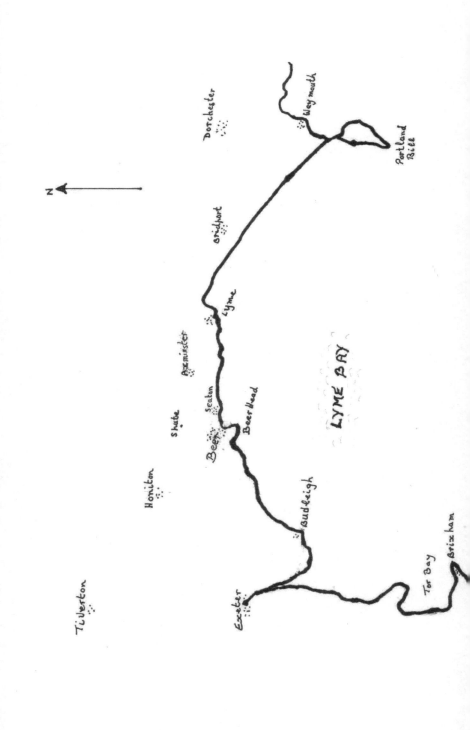

Chapter 1

The pale autumn sun slowly faded over Lyme Bay, etching the outline of a man sitting alone on the cliffs. He hunched his shoulders and winced, tentatively fingering a gash at the side of his eye while dabbing at his face distractedly with the cuff of his coarse twill shirt. A groan slipped through lips split and caked with dried blood.

What in God's name am I going to do? Jack thought. A choking sensation rose in his throat and he clenched his fists in frustration, fighting back the conviction that his wife and family would become homeless within the week.

A court bailiff had arrived at dawn and ordered his men to kick down the door of the Rattenbury family cottage. Jack had woken to the sound of splintering wood and the harsh shouts of men.

"Get out, Hannah," Jack had yelled to his wife who, screaming, had grabbed John, their youngest child, from a straw mattress beside her and made a run for the narrow backstairs.

"Gran, Gran!" John cried. His grandmother had been asleep in a cot beside the kitchen fireplace. But all exits were blocked.

"What do you want with us?" Jack had demanded.

Mr Bishop, the court officer, stood just inside the cottage door.

"I'm here with a writ demanding instant payment of outstanding debts to the Mitchell & Toms Brewery," he said, peering at Jack over the top of his glasses. He instructed his men to search the cottage.

"You leave my property alone," said Jack, pushing past the men who were rifling through drawers and throwing the contents to the floor.

The bailiff took a small ledger from his pocket, set up a tiny inkwell and began cataloguing anything of saleable value

1

in the family home. "Heavy pewter candlesticks, brass fender, solid oak dining-table..." his shrewd eyes missed nothing. He was a lean man of unimpressive stature, narrow shoulders and spindly arms, dressed in a black frock coat, shiny with age. He affected an air of studied superiority. His henchmen had been especially chosen to instil fear into debtors. Brutish, desperate men, they would stop at nothing to earn a shilling.

Not a fighting man himself, Mr Bishop delighted in the power imbued by the court and was eager to see Jack's reaction.

Jack stood with his back braced against the wall, head thrust forward from his heavy muscled shoulders. In his hand he carried a swingle bat, "Get out of here, you poxy bastard," he roared and took a wild swing in the direction of the bailiff, who stepped smartly backwards.

This is going to be more lively than I'd expected, thought Mr Bishop. "I'm afraid, Mr Rattenbury, that you may well regret this behaviour," he said, rubbing his hands.

Jack lunged towards him bellowing obscenities. With a cool nod of his head, the court officer unleashed the pack. They threw themselves onto Jack and in a second he had disappeared under the kicking, punching mob.

"Get off me, you vermin," he bellowed.

William, Jack's elder son, sprang forward but was roughly pushed aside, and for his pains received a blow to the side of his head which knocked him senseless to the floor.

Mr Bishop watched the beating impassively. He was aware, however, that his job demanded that recompense be made to the brewery and this would not be achieved if Jack were left seriously incapacitated.

"Don't kill the swine!" he shouted. His men backed off, panting heavily. "You take this as a lesson, Rattenbury. You're not above the law, despite your reputation. I'll make sure you pay your dues this time round."

The small room smelt of sweat and the heat of men filled with blood lust. Hannah, who was heavily pregnant, cowered behind the kitchen table, supported by Frances, her daughter. John escaped his mother's grasp and ran to his grandmother, who sat silently on a settle by the chimney. Anne

2

Rattenbury's back remained straight and her clear intelligent eyes watched the proceedings closely. Not for the first time was she surprised and impressed by her son's grit and determination when finding himself in trouble. Blood ran in a stream from Jack's nose and lips. William was still out cold on the floor, his face the colour of china clay. The sight of his son lying injured was enough to drive Jack into a fury but he controlled his anger and turned to the court officer.

"I give you my word you'll be paid by the end of the week." Jack had made sure throughout the debacle that the writ had not been placed in his hand, as required by law. "Just give me a week."

John had set up a steady wail of distress at the sight of his injured father and buried his head in his grandmother's skirts.

"You can see the children are suffering," said Jack. "I'll get the money to you one way or another. In the meantime, take this as surety." He went to a soot-encrusted cupboard behind the fireplace and took out a solid silver tankard bearing the words *Liberté, Egalité, Fraternité*.

Mr Bishop studied the inscription. "A laudable sentiment, I'm sure, Mr Rattenbury. I won't enquire where you obtained such a pretty piece, but I'll wager it wasn't come by legally."

Despite appearances, the bailiff had a sneaking regard for Jack. His skill as a sailor and his notorious smuggling exploits were a source of admiration from Lyme Bay to Falmouth.

"Well," he said guardedly, stroking his chin and eyeing the handsome tankard, "make sure you have the money here by next Friday night or you'll all be out on the lane with a boot up your arse." He handed the tankard to one of his assistants for safekeeping and walked out onto the Causeway. The rabble trailed behind him, already arguing over the going rate for the next job.

Silence dropped over the small, dark room for an instant and then Frances ran to William and threw a bucket of water over his head. He sat up groaning and looking dazed.

"What was all that about?" he mumbled and gently probed an angry red lump on his forehead.

Jack wiped away the blood on his mouth and stepped outside for some air. Workmen were pouring into the Causeway on their way up to the quarry; the tramp of their boots on the cobbles filled the narrow thoroughfare.

"Hope you gave as good as you got, Jack!" one of the men called out, glancing at the shattered door. "The bastards ought to get a good kickin' for that. If there's any chance of them comin' back, you let us know." There was a murmur of agreement.

Jack raised a hand in acknowledgement but avoided their eyes. The beating had left him dazed and he knelt down, plunging his face into a bucket to swill the blood off his face. His muscles tensed against the freezing water and he felt his head clear in an instant. Albert Rankin, a neighbour, sidled over. He had heard the cottage door cave in earlier and the shouted threats of the bailiff. Jack had many friends in the village, but Albert wasn't one of them.

"Sounded like they meant business, Jack. Anything I can do?" he asked.

"No thanks," said Jack, turning his back. "I can manage my own affairs." Albert was a known informer - for a small stipend he let the revenue-men know about any plans he heard for running contraband. This made him far from popular.

"That was a close call," said Hannah when Jack came back through the door. She had already taken charge, giving instructions to Frances and blowing at the fire to get the kettle on. "You better get off to work, Will, or you'll have Charlie Chapple boxin' your ears."

William quickly swallowed some ale and made off down to the boatyard without a word.

Jack's mother was sitting by the fire, comforting John and keeping him warm. "He's a tough lad, that William," she said, "just like his father." Of all the family, she seemed the least affected by the havoc.

The cottage legally belonged to Anne. It had been Jack's home since he was a child, and from the day of his marriage to Hannah, twelve years earlier, the whole family had lived

4

under the same roof. It was now too small for the growing family and it was a struggle to keep it in order.

"Look at this place," said Hannah wearily. All her lovingly polished pots and pans, together with the treasured possessions of their modest home, lay scattered about. She felt violated. "I've got to scrub that disgustin' man and his curs out of this place. Come on, Frances, get some water from the brook and we'll make a start on it."

Jack wandered around the cottage, picking things up and putting them down, unable to settle to any one task. "This is a fine kettle of fish, Mother," he said at last, sitting down by the fire. "Can't say the pub was ever a proper success but I didn't think it would come to this." Jack was close to his mother and laid great store by her opinion.

"You need to get back out to sea, Jack. That's where you do best. I know it's a hard life, but when needs must…"

Jack knew his mother was right, but his immediate worry was how to get enough money to save their home.

Hannah watched and listened. She admired Jack's mother and they managed as good a relationship as two women sharing such a cramped living space could. But Hannah had always felt that she was considered 'soft' by the older woman. She had overheard a remark made by Anne soon after her marriage that Jack should have got himself a good Beer girl, and as a result Hannah had never felt wholly accepted by her mother-in-law.

"Well, I don't feel happy about him goin' back to smuggling," said Hannah sharply, then immediately bit her tongue.

"An' who said anythin' about smugglin'?" Anne looked at her daughter-in-law and not for the first time thought she needed to toughen up.

The tension mounted as the day wore on and by mid afternoon Jack could contain himself no longer. "I'm going out for a walk over Beer Head."

His mind remained in turmoil as he made his way up towards Southdown. Looking out across the bay towards Portland, Jack could see one or two crabbers making for home, steady white plumes of spray streaming from their bows, decks piled high with pots. On the far horizon the ochre sails of the fishing luggers were scattered across the bay, their day far from over. *There's a good south-westerly to bring 'em in later*, thought Jack, his heart going out to the men, whom he knew led a hard and perilous life.

Leaving the path, he walked over to the cliffs and sat watching the boats turning towards Beer Roads. The sea looked leaden, reflecting his mood. An hour or so passed as Jack sat motionless in the fading light, stinging with humiliation from the beating he had taken and struggling to marshal his thoughts.

Chapter 2

"You all right?"

Jack raised his head and, peering through the gathering dusk, recognised an old friend, Abe Mutter. Abe was on his way back from Beer after delivering a load of turf.

"What's up, me old mate?" said Abe, leading his horse and cart up to the edge of the cliff. "Bloody hell!" he exclaimed. "You've had a bit of a pastin'."

Jack pulled a wry face. "Well, I've been doing some thinking, Abe, and it's a bugger's muddle. As far as I can see I'll have to give up the pub or I'll land up in the clink, an' that's the last thing I want."

Abe settled himself on a grassy mound and offered Jack a draw from a small flagon of cider. He had heard this story more than once in the past six months as Jack's problems with the New Inn had increased, but he let him ramble on, knowing that he needed to get it off his chest.

"I took over that pub two years back, but if truth be known I'll never make a publican," said Jack. "Thank God I only rent the place. It's the brewers; they're always on my back and any extra money I ever make, fishing or piloting, goes straight into their bloody pockets. An' another thing, you know the score, me mates are in all the time wanting grog on the slate. I haven't the heart to refuse 'em. Anyway, the brewery is takin' everythin' I've got this week, unless I can get my hands on some money."

"How much are they after?"

"Fifty guineas. It's not a fortune, but too much for me to get hold of quickly."

Abe looked thoughtful. He had known Jack since they were lads and, up until the time Jack had decided to turn his back on smuggling and try his luck as a publican, they had spent years at sea together. Suddenly he chuckled. "I was just thinking, Jack, about the scrapes we've bin in over the years.

The time you jumped off that man-o'-war was bloody amazin'! The old 'uns still talk about it."

Jack grinned, remembering a time when he had felt strong and confident. "Trouble is, Abe, the bastards are still out there and while this war's on they'll be tryin' to pick up any poor sod who can even halfway handle a boat."

"Well, I've managed to keep out of their path so far, Jack, and I'm doin' pretty well for meself. I've got runs coming in from France regular, an' the Frenchies still want to get their hands on our wool. Somebody tol' me it's for all the uniforms that swine Napoleon uses up – thousands of 'em."

"You know why I packed it in, Abe," said Jack. "Too many months locked up in poxy jails pickin' oakum while my children were growin' up, an' no father around. I had that meself as a young 'un, as you well know, an' it's not what I wanted for my own."

Abe wanted to prevent Jack going off into a gloomy reverie about his father, who had been press-ganged onto a man-of-war when Jack was a babe in arms.

"Looks to me like you haven't got too many choices, Jack," he said, "so how's this for a deal? I'll make you a loan of the money to pay off the brewery on two conditions: first, you help me out tomorrow night on a job, and second, you come in on a run to France next month. I've got a load of wool stored in the quarries, bin collecting it for ages. If we can get that over the other side and bring back a load of kegs and tea, we should be quids in. I've got three luggers goin' over an' I need somebody who knows the ropes to get us all back in one piece."

Jack stood up and stretched his legs. Looking out to sea, he was reminded of nights past, watching the cliffs for warning fires, listening for the shouts of excise men bent on snatching high rewards off the backs of others. His split and swollen lips parted in a cautious smile. Abe watched him intently, his head on one side.

"I think you're right about closing the pub," Abe told him. "A wise man knows when it's time to move on, an' that pub has never bin a good 'un."

Jack turned his head slowly and looked at Abe, weighing up his offer. *I'll never have such a chance again to set myself up,* he thought.

"You know as well as I do, Abe, that I vowed not to go back to smugglin', but if there's anybody I'd do it with, it's you. You're a cheeky varmint, and you knows what the score is, probably better than I do now."

"Not that much has changed in the last two years, Jack. Still the same old games. With this war on it's tricky, I'll give you that. The Navy is always on the look-out, pressing anybody they can get their hands on but it's either free tradin' or struggling to keep the family with a roof over their heads and good vittles in their bellies."

"What's the job for tomorrow night, Abe?"

"I've got sixty kegs comin' in from over the water. They'll be sowing the crop just below here round two o'clock, God willin'. What I'm offerin', Jack is not your usual situation, a fine seaman like yourself is better suited to 'andlin' the boats, but I've got it all set up an' can't change things around now. I'm short of a batman, an' as you know they get a bit extra, which I'm sure you could do with under the circumstances."

The highest-paid members of any smuggling gang, batmen carried weapons to protect the tub-carriers from armed customs-men.

"Fine bloody batman I'd make in this condition," said Jack, flexing his stiff shoulders. "Better hope it's a quiet night."

Abe looked out across the bay. "If it's anythin' like tonight it'll be hazy. The more sea mist the better."

"Right you are," Jack said and chuckled with anticipation. "Pass me the cider and we'll drink on it."

The evening was drawing in by the time Jack left Abe and walked back down towards the village, turning the day's events over in his mind.

Bloody amazin', he thought, philosophically. *When all looks hopeless a door opens and off I fly in another direction.* But this door would take Jack along a familiar path. His step lightened, and some of his old swagger returned as he walked down the rutted tracks of Common Lane towards Fore Street. Beer Cove nestled below, tucked into the white cliffs. A safe haven. Jack filled his lungs with the pungent reek of the beach. Never had it smelt so good. Pulling up his shirt collar against the chill wind, he turned down Sea Hill, now seething with people, and watched as one by one the luggers came in broadside on to the beach. Baskets of fish were unloaded onto the shingle and carried up to the hard. Shouted orders reached him off the shoreline.

"Lower the mainsail!"

Jack watched as the sails slid down into the boat. The crew hefted the slippery ballast stones, each weighing up to thirty pounds, and piled them on the beach, followed by trawls, masts and warps.

"Haul her up!" yelled the skipper.

Men raced to place the greased timbers as the heavy vessel was dragged up the beach on the fall of a block and tackle. Large calloused hands gripped the wet ropes as the crew hauled and strained.

"How goes it, Jack?" George Newton, another of Jack's neighbours, was sitting on a wall winging thornback skate and piling up the remains to use as bait for crab pots. "Heard you had a bit of trouble this marnin'. It's none of my business 'bout what's happened, Jack, but me and the missus want you to know that if we can help out we will."

"That's good on you, George, an' I appreciate the thought, but I hope to have things sorted by the end of this week. I've decided to close the pub and get back to sea, the quicker the better."

The old man shot Jack a glance. "I wish you well," he said, "an' you can tell Hannah that the wife will be round to help out when her time comes."

Jack slapped his neighbour on the back and walked on down the hill, happy to be part of the bustling life of the beach: fish traders driving a hard bargain, women with baskets picking up dabs to sell the next morning, children running to collect the droppings of ponies as they struggled to pull the carts, their small hooves slipping on the steep incline, up the hill and away to market.

Jack watched the familiar scene. He knew every man on the beach and every boat in sight. *Mother's right,* he thought. *The sea has always given me a living. I'd be a fool to turn me back on it.* He looked at the fishermen, their strong, stocky bodies stretched to the limit. *Get back to sea I will, but I've done enough fishin' over the years to know that it won't bring in enough to live on, at least not in any way comfortable. Just one week when the herring catch is thin can mean the family is in dire straights with no food on the table. No, much better to have more strings to me bow. Wonder how Hannah's going to take it?* He mused.

"Hannah," called Jack, his voice shattering the silence as he walked through the low door into the cottage. The room sparkled, restored to its former neatness. Hannah could not abide an untidy or dirty home and had a sharp tongue for Jack or the children if they dared come in with mucky boots or smelling of fish guts. On a hot still day the stench of fish lingered in the houses like an unwelcome visitor.

Hannah was sitting in an easy chair by the table, looking tired, but she jumped up at the sight of her husband, a smile of relief passing over her face.

"Who mended the front door?" asked Jack, examining the fresh timber. Strong deal planks had been skilfully sawn and fitted into the door frame. "Looks like they did a good job, better'n was there before," he laughed and ruffled Frances's hair. He adored his daughter and made no secret of the fact.

"Your mother went down to see Jimmy Drew," said Hannah, "an' he came straight round when he'd finished a job for Charlie Chapple." Tired as she was, Hannah knew instinctively that something was up when Jack sat down and gently placed his hand on her shoulder.

"Smells good, Mother!" he said, looking over at Anne who was frying mackerel over the fire. She had been down to the beach earlier with John, where, without a word being said, a good feed for the family had been placed in her basket.

"No, no, I won't hear of it," Mary Newton had said, when Anne held out a few coins in payment. "There's a good catch in today, plenty for all of us."

Anne hadn't argued. All the villagers, however poor, took pride in helping their own when times were hard. Well respected locally, Anne had always honoured the code, and had struggled to bring up her son without aid from the parish.

"Give this to your father," Anne said to Frances, passing over a plate of mackerel. "Looks like he could do with some sustenance."

"I've been offered a job for tomorrow night," Jack blurted out.

"Ah, I thought somethin' was up. What sort of a job?" asked Hannah.

"Well, I know we said I should keep away from smugglin', but as far as I can see there's no other way out of this mess. I've decided to close the pub. By this time next week we shall all be out on the lane unless I can get hold of some money."

Hannah shook her head. "Who came up with that idea?"

Jack was reluctant to mention Abe; in the past the pair had been notorious for their wild escapades. "I bumped into Abe Mutter up on the Common and he's offered me a deal it would be stupid to refuse," he admitted.

"Abe Mutter!" Hannah snorted. "I might have known it." Inwardly she acknowledged that it was better to be with someone who knew the game than a novice. "An' what part will you be playing in this job?"

Jack looked down at his plate, "I'm in as batman. It's not what I want to do, but there's a bit extra in it, an' it's just for this one job."

One run out as batman won't solve our problems, thought Hannah. *There's something not right about this deal. I'll have to get it out of him later.* She looked at her husband and gave a slight nod of agreement.

"That's my girl," said Jack, planting an affectionate kiss on the top of her head.

Wearily, Hannah rubbed her bulging stomach. Her pregnancy and worries about the debts they had accumulated over the past six months had taken their toll. "Once I get this one out I'll be more use round here," she sighed.

"How's our William?" asked Jack.

"Went off to work this morning as if nothin' had happened," said Hannah, "but he's got a lump on his head the size of a gull's egg."

William was serving a rough apprenticeship in Chapple's boatyard, just above the beach. Now twelve, he already felt part of the men's world.

"He's in bed if you want to see him," said Hannah.

Jack took a candle and climbed up into the attic. All the family slept in the cramped space under the thatched roof apart from Anne, who found it difficult to climb the stairs.

"What's up with you then, son?"

William was lying on a straw mattress. He pulled himself up on his elbows and looked at his father closely, trying not to laugh at his lacerated face. "What's up with you, more like?" he retorted. "You've bin like a bear with a sore head lately. An' now you've got one to show for it! After this morning I thought it'd be better to keep out of your way."

"I'm going out on a run tomorrow night with Abe Mutter," said Jack. "As you know from this morning's visit, I've got to get some money fast and that's the only way I can see of doin' it."

William stared at his father, his eyes glittering with excitement. "Can I come?" he pleaded.

"Not this time, son. It's going to be tricky by the sounds of it, and I'm goin' as batman. I may well be needin' your help in the future, though. Abe's givin' me a loan to pay off the brewers and when I've paid him back, I've a mind to get another boat." Jack paused. "That's where you come in, William. You and I could work up a good little business deliverin' cargo round the coast, an' who knows where it might go to from there," he grinned. "I don't want you involved in tradin' till you're a bit older. I've agreed with Abe to do a run next month to France, carrying wool, but don't tell your mother. With the baby comin' she's got enough to think about."

William sank back on the bed, thinking hard, his head throbbing. He had accompanied Jack on countless trips delivering cargo. The previous year he had been aboard a boat returning from Alderney when it broke up in heavy seas, but the lad had coped well and kept his head.

"In the meantime, William, you take care of your mother. It's goin' to be a hard few weeks."

Downstairs, Hannah sat staring into the fire.

"You look done in, girl," said Anne, pouring Hannah a noggin of brandy from a small store she kept behind the chimney.

"What do you think about this deal, Mother?" she said.

"As you know, Hannah, I like to keep my nose out of your business, but it seems to me that Jack's got no choice. I think it likely that Abe's putting up the money to pay off the brewery," said Anne. "He's not one to miss a chance to get Jack back into tradin'. You got to accept it, Hannah, most of the men round here makes ends meet by a mixture of smuggling and fishing. It's a fact of life. I know it's not what you're used to, but that's the way it is."

Hannah sighed. She knew that Anne spoke the truth. She had never regretted leaving Lyme and marrying Jack, but the bad times were not easily shrugged off. He had been in gaol several times during their marriage and it was only by his quick wits and through the patronage of the local aristocracy that he had regained his freedom.

"Well, I believe there should be another way to earn enough money to support a family in a law-abiding way," she said. Although, resourceful as she was, she could not think of one. "This time I'm going to keep behind Jack, and if you're right about the deal and the pub debts are paid off, I'll find a way out of this trap."

The stair door opened and Jack walked back into the kitchen.

"I've been talking things over with your mother," Hannah told him firmly, "an' I want you to know that I'm not at all happy about this job with Abe Mutter."

Jack sat down in the chair. "Well, what else would you suggest?"

"I don't know, but there must be some way a man can make an honest livin' without risking life and limb. Your mother's of the opinion that Abe is paying off the debt at the brewery to get you back working with him."

Jack looked at Anne and smiled. "You don't miss much, do you, Mother?" he said. " Anyway, so what, Hannah! I'm still a free agent when it's paid back, that's how I see it. Just look round this village. Eight to ten shillings a week is all you can expect to earn farm labourin' or workin' in the quarry, an' you know full well that I've tried piloting and fishing, but it's still bloody difficult to keep our heads above water. The pub going down was the last straw."

Hannah eased her aching body against the chair. *Just wait till I get my strength back. He won't get away with things so easily,* she thought. "Time for bed," she said. "I don't want any more days like this one."

Jack stood up and looked in a small mirror hanging beside the window. "Just look at my face," he said. Handsome was not a word to describe Jack. His skin was weather-beaten and bore the scars of years at sea facing the elements. His charm and attraction lay in his dark brown eyes and ready smile. Those who didn't know him well would have been hard put to discover his kind and gentle nature, well concealed beneath a bluff and roguish humour.

Hannah pulled herself up out of her chair and went to stand beside her husband. "You'll live," she said gently, stroking his hair.

Jack smiled as he examined his swollen eye. The spark between them remained. (Even Anne had to acknowledge that, despite her reservations, Hannah was a good wife and mother.)

"Let's just get the next few weeks over," said Jack, rubbing Hannah's back.

Jack had agreed to meet Abe early the following morning to discuss the details of the run and to pick up the weapons he needed. Although he had never worked as batman in a smuggling gang, over the years he had run many boats in which they were employed. Batmen were usually as hard as nails, able to kill and maim without remorse. Jack did not consider himself soft, and could fight with the best of them, but he had always preferred to avoid violent confrontations if at all possible.

Jack left the cottage just before dawn, well aware that the eyes and ears of some in the village would be alert. In order to avoid suspicion he set out up Long Hill as if to walk to Seaton, meaning to cut back over the fields to Bovey Cross and meet up with Abe on the slopes of Peak Hill, near Sidmouth.

Although it was early, Long Hill was busy. As it was Thursday, large blank-eyed cows were plodding up through the village, churning up the rutted tracks, on their way to Axminster market.

"Hup hup!" shouted the farm lads, landing sharp slaps on the rumps of the lumbering animals, who managed a short trot before dropping back to a steady plod. Their warm breath ballooned out into the cold morning air and mingled with the pungent smell of warm dung and the stench of the open drain running down the narrow gully beside the lane.

Men on their way to the quarries greeted Jack every few steps. "Marnin', Jack. You all right?"

He responded with a friendly wave and strode on purposefully, not stopping to make idle conversation. At the top of the hill he paused to get his breath. *God, I'm out of fettle,* he thought, *I'd better get rid of this beer gut quick.*

He looked down over the village, set deep in a narrow winding coomb below him, with a strong sense of loyalty and affection. Wood smoke from chimneys drifted up the narrow valley, and dogs barked, guarding their territory. The view out to sea was clear; the rising sun, still below the horizon, cast a sheen of liquid silver over the water.

Chapter 3

After Jack had left, Hannah lay in bed mulling over the events of the previous day. *It's going to take more than this one job,* she thought. But she couldn't fault him accepting the offer of a loan. *When Jack's paid that off, we'll have to see if we can get our hands on a boat. I'd feel better if Jack could skipper his own and not be beholden to anybody else.* She rolled out of bed and pulled on some clothes against the chill. It was time to get William up for work. Her body felt heavy and slow, making her irritable and ready for a row. Climbing down the steep staircase, she found that Anne already had a good fire going in the hearth.

"William, get out of that bed!" Hannah shouted.

The two women were surprised when the boy jumped downstairs in one bound, brimful of energy and high spirits. He kept his head down while swallowing his ale and bread. "I know what you've been talking to your father about," Hannah said sternly. "You're getting a good training down at the yard, an' we need the money you're bringin' in now, so don't you get carried away with his ideas. You listen to me, William, and just remember the time he's spent behind bars."

"I'm off," said William. "Send a message down to the yard if you need me."

William walked down towards the beach flexing his shoulders. He had Jack's build, short stocky legs, wide shoulders and a broad back. He was proud of his strength and took a delight in showing off around the village. "You can tell he's Rattenbury's son," snickered some behind his back. *I don't care what she says,* thought William. *I'm going to start working with Father. We've got to get another boat and set up on our own. One good run with a load of kegs and we'd be well set up. I'll keep my eyes open for a likely craft.* Reaching the top of Sea Hill he scanned the bay. The luggers' sails could be seen in the far distance making for Torbay. The beach looked empty without them, the only boats remaining being those in need of repair. William cast an appraising eye over them and resolved to talk to his father at the first opportunity.

After William's noisy departure, Anne looked at Hannah and shook her head. "There's no holdin' 'em back, Hannah. All you can do is say your piece, but if they don't want to hear it, then so be it. William's got a lot of his father in him, an' by the time Jack was William's age he'd bin at sea for near on three years."

The rigid line of her daughter-in-law's mouth told her any further discussion was pointless. "I'm goin' down to the beach this marnin'," she said. "It was good of Mary Newton to help us yesterday, but we can't expect handouts every day. Maybe I can get some fish off the boats to sell round the village."

"All right, Mother," said Hannah. "I'll get the others up now, and send John down a bit later."

John was never happier than with his grandmother. They spent many hours talking to the fishermen on the beach and buying fish to sell at the top of Sea Hill. Anne had taught him to shout their wares, standing on a wooden crate: "Fresh fish, come an' get your fresh fish here." His reedy voice would rise above the clattering of carts on the cobbles and cries of the sea-birds wheeling overhead. Most people would laugh and pass on but some would stop and buy a few dabs or a mackerel.

Anne wrapped a thick woollen shawl around her shoulders and covered her head with a knitted bonnet. Picking up a wicker fish basket outside the cottage door, she set off down the path.

Hannah busied herself in the kitchen, then roused Frances and John.

"I want you to gather up a good pile of wood today, Frances. An' before you do that you can take John down the beach to his grandmother." She stirred a handful of oats into some hot water and topped it with a splash of milk. "Here, take this. It's cold this morning and you'll want somethin' in your belly."

Frances, now eight years old, was a sturdy, hard-working child, and enjoyed collecting wood. She had a good many friends her age around the village and they would meet at the bottom of Fore Street for the walk up to the Common.

"Here's a bit of bread to put in your pocket," said Hannah.

Frances and John didn't always see eye to eye and Frances often gave him a clipped ear when out of his mother's sight.

The cottage was now quiet and Hannah brushed her dark hair into a smooth bun at the back of her head and pulled on her cloak, which only just covered her advanced condition. The wooden yoke, which supported two buckets, was hanging on the wall outside the cottage and picking it up, she walked slowly down the Causeway to collect the water. By now the men were in the quarries, on the farms or out at sea and the only people on the lanes were men past working age, women and children.

Hannah was aware of the crowd of women along the lane; she steeled herself to meet their nosy questions.

"You look about to burst your britches," said one. "When's your time?"

"It can't come soon enough for me," Hannah replied, forcing a smile. "Next week, probably. I shall be needin' some help from Alice."

A self-taught midwife, Alice Chapple attended most confinements in the village. The women waited, hoping that Hannah would provide them with some juicy details of the bailiff's raid. But she maintained her silence and walked on, ignoring the whispers and barely concealed smirks. At the stream, Hannah was relieved to see some close friends.

"Hear Jack's having a bit of bother," said Jane Bartlett, a near neighbour of Hannah's. She squeezed her arm in a gesture of support.

Hannah paused, conscious that the chatter had stopped. "Yes, we've decided to close the pub," she said clearly.

"Couldn't make a go of it, and anyway, Jack's better off at sea. Seems like that's where he's happiest."

"I heard the bailiff's men gave him a hard time," said a woman called Sarah Wild.

Hannah stared into the woman's mocking eyes and threw her head back. "Well, nobody can say that Jack can't take it. He was back on his feet in no time." And keeping her back straight and her face composed, she waited her turn at the conduit.

"Just ask if I can do anything," said Jane Bartlett quietly. She had been in many scrapes with Hannah over the years. "We'll walk back up home together, an' I'll give you a hand with the water."

Hannah nodded her gratitude and lifted the heavy wooden yoke on to her shoulders. *That's the first hurdle over*, she thought. She knew that it was safe to confide in Jane. Her husband was a fisherman but out of necessity frequently supplemented the family income by crewing on smuggling runs.

"The last two years have been quieter," said Hannah, "but looks like Jack's rarin' to get back to his old ways. Is Jim in on this run tonight?"

"That he is, Hannah, an' I'm up on the cliffs keepin' watch with Ruth. I heard that Jack is on as batman, an' that can be a bit rough. Let's hope there's no bother. But don't worry, your business is safe with me, Jim told me all about it this marnin'."

Hannah smiled. "You're a good friend, Jane, an' I appreciate it. No doubt I'll be back up there alongside you in a couple of weeks."

Chapter 4

It took Jack a good three hours to reach Peak Hill, where he found Abe loading turf onto a cart. The men greeted each other warmly.

"I'll give you the bones of it," said Abe. "We need to get round to Hooken Beach just before midnight. I'll row out to the mooring with two runners and Matt Westlake, who knows, to the yard, where the kegs are lying. There's near on sixty of 'em. It's going to take some doing gettin' that lot ashore, but I'll have thirty tub-carriers waitin' on the beach. You're the only batman, so you'll need to keep your eyes peeled. If we're lucky it will be clear enough to see the cork markers, an' there should be enough sea mist up by then not to be spotted from the bay."

Abe handed Jack a swingle bat and a boarding blunderbuss wrapped in oilcloth. "Have you used one of these?"

Jack handled the gun gingerly. "I've been around 'em enough to know that they be tricky to handle, particularly on a boat when it's bouncing round a bit. But never you mind about that, Abe, I'll manage one way or t'other."

"I've got a couple of look-outs on Beer Head," said Abe. "It's the Bartlett women, if you want to know, and bloody good they are too. Absolutely fearless! When we're all ashore the carriers will be up the Undercliff path and on to the Common in about twenty minutes. You'll need eyes in the back of your head, guarding the beach and the path until we're clear. Once we're up the top there's always the possibility of a riding officer comin' up from Branscombe. So, as I said, keep your eyes open. It's goin' to be a busy night, an' that's why we're not using the caves. Three more luggers are comin' in later. We want this load away fast to Bovey House. I'll have a string of ponies waiting on the common and they should be into the lanes in no time."

Jack listened carefully. Familiar with this run and all the problems it posed, he knew that, this time, he would be the weak link in the chain.

"How much is in it for me?" He asked.

"The going rate's twelve shillings all in for a batman, and if we pull it off I'll make sure you get extra. But remember the deal, Jack. This is just the beginning. The money to pay off the brewery will be with you on Thursday evening."

"Right, Abe. I'll be on the beach before midnight and in the meantime I'll keep my ears pricked. The village is crawling with dragoons, all of 'em eager to win their stripes." He stowed the bat and the blunderbuss in a sack, covering the weapons with bundles of firewood.

Jack returned to Beer along the cliffs, checking the route the tub-carriers would be using and looking to ensure that the ponies were in the right spot. The common stretched down to a farm above the village. Sheep grazed perilously near the cliff edge and donkeys laden with fish and potatoes trotted along Middle Path. Jack waved as he caught sight of his daughter collecting firewood with her friends.

"Hey up, Frances!" The youngsters' faces, red from the cold, lit up with smiles. Jack was popular with the local children, who viewed him with a mixture of affection and awe.

The ponies stood nearby, grazing peacefully. Small, tough and sure-footed, they were bred for load-carrying. But Jack knew from experience they could be vicious, and few excise men would dare approach them head on. *Looks like Abe has got it well organised,* thought Jack, forcing himself to relax a little and enjoy the walk. He felt better after a night's sleep. Looking out across the bay to Portland and watching the steady roll of the sea, he gloried in the view and relished the thought that soon he would be out there, back in his element again.

Arriving in Beer, Jack concealed the bag containing the gun in the cottage and made his way down through the village to the beach. He could see William working in the boatyard.

"How's it goin', Will?" Jack shouted. William looked up and gave a quick wave. He knew better than to stop work:

he would get a cuff around the ear from Charlie, who was a hard task-master. The yard was bustling with activity. Partly finished boats stood on stocks; men and boys crawled over them like ants, sawing, hammering, and laying thick layers of tar along the timbers. Jack had his reasons for going to the yard: he wanted to broadcast the message that he was back on his feet and fighting fit, and also to have a look at the boats.

"Hey, Charlie, got anythin' useful in?" he asked.

Charlie looked up, and walked over, brushing sawdust out of his hair. He was a big man, renowned for his superhuman strength and short temper.

"Well, I've a good-sized sloop in for repair, the *Volante*. If I remember rightly, Jack, you're familiar with her."

"That I am, Charlie, but that was a few years back. What sort of shape is she in now?" The two men climbed into the boat and began a thorough inspection. A large hole near the bow, caused by a collision with a cutter, was in the process of repair, but Jack could see that the sturdy oak frame and the mast were intact, and he knew that most other things on a sloop could be repaired cheaply.

He shook his head. "There's a bit of work to do there," he said, "an' the sails could do with some attention."

"Well, I'll have her good as new in a couple of months," said Charlie, casually sliding open a large storage locker concealed behind the bulkhead. Nothing was said but the message was clear.

"Whose name is she in now?"

"That I can't rightly say, Jack. All I know is that the owner is sellin' a half-share in her.

"I may be interested, Charlie, so don't let her go before talking to me." With that, Jack strolled down to the beach for a chat with some of his mates. The day was closing in and the fishing boats were heading back into the cove.

Chapter 5

That night, Jack left the cottage at a quarter to midnight, his face half-hidden by a handkerchief and his boots muffled with sacking. Abe was right: the sky was overcast, the lane wrapped in an inky blackness. Jack slipped silently over the cobbles, keeping close to the walls, as he made his way down through the village. After Ponds Wall he passed the boat yard and made his way over to a small promontory on the right-hand side of the beach. The only sound was the running brook and the whish of gentle waves rattling over the pebbles.

"Hey up!" a voice whispered. A dark shape moved out from the shadows. Matt Westlake clapped Jack across the shoulders.

"Good to have you with us, Jack," he said softly. "It's going to be a hard night, but so far it's been quiet enough."

The cliffs towered above their heads like a church. They could just make out King's Hole rock on the opposite side of the beach, but mist clung on the outer reaches of the bay.

Behind Matt stood two figures, both masked. Jack had no idea who the men were. He assumed Abe had recruited them in Sidmouth. No one spoke. Jack could smell the fear. They all knew that to be caught would mean lost years when they would not see their friends and family, or know the comfort of a familiar bed.

Matt raised his head. "Sounds like Abe's comin' across," he said. The creak of oars could be heard across the water as Abe manoeuvred his boat into the shore. The men climbed aboard. They rowed towards Hooken, hugging the cliffs and making sure to avoid the jagged rocks of the Great Ledge.

Jack sat at the back of the boat scanning the cliffs and out to sea. The gun lay by his side primed and ready to fire. Just one flash of light off Beer Head would have the run scuppered.

Within fifteen minutes the small boat had turned the headland. Matt was looking for a point about a hundred yards offshore; he hung over the side of the boat and stared at the inky water. The mooring was fixed, using the triangulation of Castle Rocks and Beer Head. "There they be, nice little beauties," he muttered and silently held up his hand. The oarsmen hove to. Floating beside the boat were lines of corks.

"Haul em in!" ordered Abe in a harsh whisper. "We should get twenty kegs in if we squeeze up. That makes three trips. Get moving!"

Jack kept watch while the four men struggled to pull the slippery dripping kegs into the boat.

"Right, that's it boys," said Abe, when the first twenty were counted in, "let's get 'em in quick." They rowed hard towards the beach. It looked deserted, but as soon as the boat hit the shingle, masked men ran from the shadows to hold it steady and unload.

It was a slick operation and the first ten carriers were making for the narrow track off the beach leading to the cliff path as the boat left the shore for the next load. The men were nimble and sure-footed as ponies. Each carried two kegs in a harness which held one keg on his chest and one on his back. They could earn more in a night as a tub-carrier than in a week on the farm.

Jack left the beach after the first load and followed the dark snake of climbing men up the path. The only sound came from their labouring breath and the swish of scrub against their legs. Jack was conscious of his heart, hammering in protest at the steep gradient. Sweat ran down his tortured face, dripping off his chin. When he reached the bend in the Undercliff path he hunkered down under a rock overhang. There was a clear view down to the beach and up to the top of the path where the ponies stood waiting on the Common. *This will be the one and only time I work as batman,* he vowed to himself.

Two more loads were brought up and when the last man left the beach Jack climbed up towards the Common, pausing briefly to watch Matt push the boat off. The plan was to row back to the moorings and pull up some lobster pots, set earlier in the week, before returning to Beer

Jack wearily pushed himself to his feet as the last tub-carrier left the path. By now the front ponies would be loaded and ready for the last leg. As he walked up to the group a scuffle broke out between Abe and the lead carrier who was demanding the rate be increased.

"This has been a bloody long night's work," he argued. "We were told it would only take two hours and we've been here three already." He looked menacing and ready for a fight.

Jack raised the blunderbuss, hoping he wouldn't need to use it. "Get these ponies movin' or you'll get nothin'," he said quietly.

The man looked at Jack's face and despite the mask, knew in an instant who he was.

"It's not bloody right," he muttered, but Jack could see he had the upper hand and kept right behind him, the gun aimed at his back. The silent troop of men and ponies set off through the lanes, where the hedgerows closed around them into long dark tunnels. Jack went ahead, keeping to the shadows, all his senses on full alert.

After half an hour or so they reached an avenue of poplar trees standing like sentinels and in the distance Bovey House sat in silent crumbling splendour. The owner, Lord Rolle, was rarely in residence and appeared to turn a blind eye to the use smugglers made of his estate.

Jack walked lightly up the avenue followed by the line of men and ponies. The house was known to the excise men who had lain in ambush there before. Every man strained to hear the first sign of an impending attack or, perhaps even worse, a glimpse of the ghost, said to inhabit the grounds. They stopped at the well, standing close to the walls of the house, its mouth gaping and ominous.

"Will, where are you?" Abe whispered. "Come on, lad, we got to get movin'."

Will stepped forward, a slight young man, little more than a boy. His job was to be lowered down into the well in the basket and roll the kegs out when it came alongside the hidden room. The ropes creaked as the basket slipped below the rim. The dank slimy walls closed in around Will and he struggled to stay his fears and control his chattering teeth. It took more than twenty loads but finally the kegs were stowed and Will was hauled up for the last time.

"Glad that's over," he muttered as he crawled over the rim of the well. His thin, ill-nourished body shook with fright.

Abe looked relieved, but he would not rest easy until every last man was home and safe in bed. "Looks like this is goin' to be a straight forward run tonight", he said. Along the way he had decided to split the difference with the tub-carriers. He needed their co-operation and there was no point in making enemies.

"Right," he said when all the kegs were safely stacked. "Here's your money and somethin' extra for doing a good job. We're loading at the quarries next month. I'll get word to you if there's any changes."

The bonus would make life easier for the tub-carriers in the coming week and they needed no encouragement to slip away, leaving Will and young George Bray to return the ponies to the Common, ready for the next run.

"Well, that was a new trick for you, Jack," said Abe.

By now Jack had got his breath back and was able to laugh at his clumsy attempt as batman. "Handling boats is more to my likin', Abe, and guns are not my weapon of choice. I'd rather use me fists or wits to get out of tight corners."

"Some things have changed a bit, Jack, while you've bin out of the business. The bloody excise men and riding officers are everywhere and well armed into the bargain. Anyway, here's five guineas to tide you over. The rest will be with you on Thursday night."

The money felt good in Jack's pocket. *This is what makes it worthwhile*, he thought.

"We need to get together to talk over the next run," said Abe. "It's goin' to be a totally different operation. I've got the three luggers signed up for it, but loadin' all that wool is goin' to be bloody hard."

Jack reached the Causeway just as the first streaks of dawn lightened the eastern sky.

Hannah had had a restless night waiting for Jack's return. When the back door closed with a soft thud she slipped downstairs. "Thank God you're back in one piece, I've hardly slept."

"It went smooth as a bottle," whispered Jack, anxious not to wake his sleeping mother. "Abe had everythin' thought-out and we were lucky enough to choose a quiet night. No sign of the excise anywhere. Here, this helps doesn't it?" Jack spilled the coins into her hand.

"Five guineas," said Hannah. "How did you get that much?"

"Tell you tomorrow," yawned Jack. "I feel proper knocked out now."

Hannah pursed her lips. *Patience*, she cautioned herself and gave Jack a mug of ale with some bread and cheese.

"I'm goin' back up to see if I can get an hour's sleep," she said.

Jack followed her and was soon sleeping soundly.

Chapter 6

Shortly after 5a.m. Hannah jerked awake. A sharp, urgent pain gripped her stomach and slid around to the base of her back, where it settled with stubborn determination, sinking deep into her spine. She gasped and pulled herself upright. Jack slept on, oblivious.

Hope this isn't a false alarm, she thought, but within minutes the next spasm gathered with increasing force. A low moan escaped through her gritted teeth. She swung her legs over the edge of the bed and made her way over to where Frances lay sleeping.

"Frances," she whispered, shaking her daughter awake. "Run an' get Mrs Chapple and wake your grandmother. Tell her to get the fire goin'."

Frances rubbed the sleep out of her eyes and, feeling all fingers and thumbs, pulled on her boots and smock. In two jumps she was down the stairs.

"Wake up, wake up, Granny, the baby's comin'! Mother said to get the fire goin'." Frances grabbed her shawl and ran down through the deserted village to lower Fore Street, where Alice Chapple's cottage stood a little way back from the brook.

Hannah crept down the narrow stairs, holding on to the wall.

"Come an' sit here, Hannah," said Anne. "I'll get you a drop of brandy with some hot water." The two women sat in a tense but companionable silence.

"Looks like I'll have to use your bed, Mother. I'll not get back up those stairs tonight," said Hannah, going over to the cot tucked into a cramped alcove by the fire.

Anne blew on the glowing coals and soon had a blaze going. It sent a flickering light around the room and shadows danced on the low smoke-stained ceiling. "I'll get some hot water goin' for Alice," she said, placing a pan on the iron trivet.

Hannah sat back, breathing heavily. She was glad she had spent the day cleaning, and gazed around the neat and shining cottage with a sense of satisfaction.

The minutes stretched into half an hour; Hannah stood up and roamed around the room, every now and then pausing to grip the back of a chair for support. Sweat beaded her forehead. "If it's a girl, I want to name her after you, Mother."

Anne looked up and smiled, her rough hard-working hands folded in her lap. "Well if it is, Hannah, I would wish her an easier life than mine. It's been hard since John was taken. I did meet one other, when Jack was a boy, but he soon disappeared after the baby died." Anne rarely mentioned her second child's father, but he was thought to have been a local fisherman.

Hannah walked slowly over to the bed and lay down. "It's not far off now, Mother," her voice rose in apprehension. "I can tell. Where can Alice have got to?" she said irritably, holding her stomach and grimacing as another powerful wave gripped her body.

At that moment the door flew open and Alice Chapple billowed through the doorway, closely followed by Frances.

"Don't you worry, my dear," said Alice, taking in Hannah's distraught face at a glance. "We'll soon get you sorted out. Have you got the kettle on, Anne?" she asked, smiling at Jack's mother. "I shall need you in a minute. An' Frances, you get the young 'un back into his bed. We don't need him around."

Frances turned to see John sitting on the bottom step. "Upstairs now," she said, pushing him up the stairs. Frances retained a dim memory of John's birth, which had taken place in the upstairs room and now she was struggling with a mixture of fear and intense curiosity.

"Won't take long by the looks of it," said Alice, her arms buried in Hannah's voluminous nightdress.

Anne supported Hannah's head as she groaned and thrashed about the narrow bed.

"Oh, God help me!" wailed Hannah

Alice gave her a piece of rolled linen to bite on and urged her to bear down. At last, with one long drawn-out cry,

Hannah pushed another Rattenbury into the world. She sank back onto the bed exhausted.

The thin insistent cry of the newborn baby filled the room. After a quick look, to check that all was well, Alice wrapped the wriggling wet bundle in a square of cotton and handed her to Frances.

Alice laughed. "Close your mouth, girl, you know what it's all about now, don't you! Just give her a quick wash over and keep her warm." Alice busied herself with cleaning Hannah up. "I'll just throw this in the brook," she said, picking up a wooden slop bucket standing by the bed, and then I'll be off."

The door closed, leaving the three Rattenbury women to welcome baby Ann into the family.

Jack stood looking down into the cot. "Not another daughter!" he said. It was now late morning and Hannah was up and sitting at the table. She was delighted to have a second daughter and sat cradling the newborn, savouring her sweet smell and softly kissing her neck.

Hannah gave Jack a straight look and he knew that this time she would not be fobbed off. "Jack, I want to know what's goin' on."

"If you feel up to it I'd like to talk it over," said Jack. "I've been mulling over a couple of possibilities. You must understand, Hannah, that it's goin' to take a few months of free trading to get us clear of the debt to Abe, an' in the meantime, I'll be working out how to set myself up with a boat. I've been talking to Charlie about the *Volante*. You remember I worked on her with Will Loveridge out of Lyme a few years back? She's bin around a while, but she's sound enough. Had a bang from an excise cutter, an' Charlie's repairing her down the yard. Somebody, although Charlie wouldn't say who, wants to sell a half share and is lookin' to find a working partner."

Hannah perked up. "Who'd you think that might be?" Her nimble mind ran quickly through the possibilities.

Jack grinned. "Who knows? There's plenty of gentry round Devon with money invested in trading vessels."

Hannah stroked the baby's head and looked thoughtful. "Well, if it's Lord Rolle he wouldn't support anything illegal, but there's plenty of work shifting cargo."

"I s'pose so," said Jack, privately thinking that his lordship might well be interested in a few other uses a good boat could be put to. "Right," he went on. "It looks like we agree on the way forward, but the next few months are going to be hard and risky. Abe has fixed up a run over the water next month. It's a big job with three luggers goin'. I'll have me hands full but it'll pay well. One thing you can do is keep your ears open around the village and see if there's wind of it, an' the same with you, Mother. No doubt Albert Rankin will be watching me like a hawk."

Hannah looked at Jack and felt an overwhelming wave of affection. *We're a good team,* she thought and handed the baby to Frances. "God, I feel tired," she said, suddenly feeling faint with exhaustion.

Chapter 7

On Thursday night, Jack met up with Abe, who handed him a bag containing the fifty guineas.

"I'm bloody grateful for this, Abe. I'll have you know that I'll be working like a dog for the next few months to get this paid off and after that, God willing, I'll be able to get a vessel." Jack had decided to wait until he was in a stronger financial position before telling Abe that he was interested in acquiring a share in the *Volante*.

"So we're back free trading?" said Abe, smiling broadly. Jack let that go and moved on to other business.

When William came home that evening Jack suggested they take a walk around the fields. William was curious, but knew better than to ask questions. In the fading light they set off up the lane, busy with men making their way home from the quarries and surrounding farms. Some of the younger men were in high spirits, joking with friends, but most walked with a steady lope, weary after long hours of labour.

Leaving the lane, Jack stepped through the bushes onto a narrow concealed track leading up over the bank. Under the trees it was dark but Jack knew the path intimately.

"I cut this path out with Abe before you could walk, Will, but I don't want you tellin' anyone about it, not even your mother."

At a small cleft in the rocks, Jack stopped and listened. The dusk had quickly deepened into night and the woods closed in around them. Apart from the rustling of nesting birds and disturbed rabbits nothing moved.

"I expect you'll want to know what's up." Jack kept his voice low.

William waited, secretly delighted that his father was confiding in him.

"Abe an' me are takin' a load of wool across to France next month. It's stacked in one of the old workings back of the quarries. I just want to take a look at it. Got to get the loading right, wool can be bloody heavy if it gets wet."

William listened intently, "How many blokes is it going to take to get it onto the beach?"

Jack paused. He hadn't had much experience of "owling", as wool smuggling was known, but had gathered from Abe that it would weigh around three tons.

"Probably take 'round fifty, some loading, some handling the ponies. I'll be down on the beach with three luggers ready to launch. So nobody'll be slackin'."

William nodded gravely. "Wish I could help."

"Take it from me, William, when this war's over there'll be no call for our wool in France, so it'll be best for us to spread our interests in future."

They carefully picked their way through to a gap in the rocks and followed an old cart-track into a large cavern. Dark tunnels led off in several directions. Jack lit a small candle, which gave off a flicker of light. Unworked for years, this part of the quarry was ideal for storing contraband. Water seeped through cracks in the roof and collected in pools on the floor and early hibernating bats could be seen clustering in the crevices.

William shivered. "This is a bloody creepy place, Father."

The bales of wool stood against the walls, covered in oiled cloth.

"God, what a stink! It's like having your nose up a sheep's arse!" said William, finding an excuse to leave and get out into the fresh air.

Jack followed, laughing quietly. "You may turn your nose up, son, but that stink's worth a small fortune. Let's get home, I need to get some food in my belly and a bit of sleep, I'm up early fishin'."

As they neared the cottage Albert Rankin walked up the lane towards them, holding a lantern. William brushed roughly past him, causing the man to stumble into the gutter.

"Rat," he hissed into Albert's startled face.

Jack glared at William and, grabbing his collar, pushed him into the front garden. "Get indoors, you idiot," he hissed sharply. "We don't want to attract attention from the likes of him, so keep your mouth shut."

Albert and his wife, Dora, were treated with contempt by the Rattenbury family. Hannah would walk past him in the lane as if he was invisible. The children followed their parents' example, adding their own particular brand of insults: knocks on the window after dark, lumps of dog-shit left on the front doorstep, sly whisperings and mocking laughter.

The weeks passed quickly and on the first Friday in November, as agreed with Abe, Jack slipped out of the house well before midnight and made for the beach. In the hills behind the village the ponies were being led to the concealed quarry entrance, their hooves wrapped in sacking. The air in the cavern was thick with the smell of horse sweat, raw wool and the fear of the carriers. Bale after bale was lashed onto the ponies' backs under the flames of small candles flickering in clay cups, set back in the walls.

Abe pursed his lips, making the soft hoot of an owl, the signal that the last pony had left the cave and was moving down into the lane.

Jack stood waiting at the water's edge. In the starlight he saw the dark shapes of the ponies as they picked their way down Sea Hill. In hushed tones he discussed the course with the two other skippers. As the luggers were loaded Jack watched like a hawk. "I want the boats evenly stowed or we'll know it if a storm hits us," he told the crew.

The carriers strained and heaved the bales off the backs of the ponies, who stood uncomplaining and steady as rocks. By now the men were tiring. It was past midnight and most had started work at first light on farms or in the quarries. They ran to and fro, the wet slippery pebbles sliding beneath their feet. No one stirred in the fishermen's cottages clinging to the cliffs opposite Charlie's boatyard and if anyone heard the ponies, none would dare open their doors.

The boats were loaded and ready to go within the hour; the cargo wedged in tight below the gunnels. Jack called the skippers together to tell them of a change of plan.

"I've decided to head south of Cherbourg to Omonville. It's best to steer clear of Cherbourg harbour: too many privateers and men-o'-war around for my liking."

The skippers looked surprised but they trusted Jack's judgement implicitly.

"When we get within five miles I'll pull ahead and lead you into the bay," Jack went on. "Looks like we've got a north-westerly, which, should it last out, will get us there in about twelve hours."

The men listened respectfully. They were both skilled seamen, but Jack could use his experience and cunning in ways which left most men floundering.

"We'll leave together, then. Should any of you be spotted in the Channel, just scatter. The signal will be two shots from a musket. They can't chase all of us. See you in Omonville, gentlemen." Jack shook hands with the skippers and promised them a good feed and plenty of wine when they reached safe haven.

As the first lugger left the beach heading for Beer Roads, Abe turned to Jack standing on the shore. "Good idea of ours to save naming the place until just before leaving," he told him. "Can't be too careful. I'd like to be coming with you but I've got to get the carriers and transport arranged for when you get back. You've got a good crew with Jim Bartlett an' Sam. They knows the ropes. God willin', the wind'll stay in your favour."

Jack nodded. "An' fingers crossed this Louis Claude bloke keeps his side of the bargain and has the Frog carriers organised. I know to my cost that they can be unreliable."

The remaining carriers pushed Jack's lugger off the sloping beach and disappeared into the night. Jack looked at the mast in satisfaction, watching the lugsail fill as the boat surged forward. He never tired of hitting the water and heading out to the open sea powered by a good north-west wind. Ahead of him he could see the outline of the two leading boats, their bows ploughing steadily through the waves.

Five hours out into the Channel a light fog crept in from the east, drifting over the water like a wraith.

"What's that?" said Tom, one of the crew. Tom was just twelve years of age. The muffled ring of a bell reached them through the mist and within a mile the lights of a vessel could be seen on the port side. Jack wore the foresail round and the lugger pulled to starboard.

"Who might that be, Mr Rattenbury?" whispered Tom.

Jack checked the compass and grunted. "Could have been a cargo boat going into Lyme. Unlikely to have been an excise cutter, they don't like to signal their whereabouts."

Minutes ticked by into hours with no further sightings. As the first pale threads of light touched the horizon Jack hauled in a line and landed six good-sized dog mackerel. "These should quieten our bellies for a bit, with a brew and a tot of brandy. Gets the blood moving. Here, Tom, get the fire goin' an' get these fish gutted."

"Any more brandy in that there keg, Jack?" asked Sam, an older crew member who had known Jack since he was a lad. "My bones is frozen solid."

Jack laughed, "You're getting soft, Sam. I remember when you could sail through the night in a force ten an' make nothin' of it. There's just a noggin, an' you shall 'ave it, since you'se the oldest here."

Within four hours the coast of Normandy appeared on the horizon. Wooded hills rolled gently into the hinterland from a shoreline edged with sandy coves. They were to drop their cargo seven sea miles south of Cherbourg; the cliffs gave excellent cover from cruising privateers and the villagers were not averse to a spot of free trading with the English. Jack watched through his spyglass as children from the village raced along the shore, their bare feet flying over the sand.

"They've been waiting for the red sails," he said to Tom, who was watching the line and fearful of hearing the keel hit the rocks. Jack carefully plumbed the lead and took the three luggers through a small channel lying off the broad sandy beach. As they hove to, he signalled the skippers to drop anchor while he went ashore in a small tender, accompanied by two armed batmen.

A tall white-haired man standing on the shore watched Jack step onto the beach and raised his hand in salute.

"Bonjour, Monsieur Rattenbury. Bienvenue," he said.

Jack looked amazed. "Ah Monsieur Claude, je suis content de vous voir encore." said Jack, in halting French. "It must be nigh on eighteen years since we last met, an' we both have some grey hair to show for it."

The Frenchman looked at him with affection. Jack drew himself up and stepped back.

"So many years to catch up on, Monsieur Claude, but first we have business to complete," he said. "Three tons of raw wool we've got here to unload and stinking stuff it is too, but no doubt it's good quality."

As he spoke, a gang of around fifty armed men arrived on the beach leading pack-mules. Their leader stared at Jack, a mixture of contempt and arrogance on his swarthy face. His lips contorted into a sneer.

"English scum," he muttered. His men grinned and laughed.

"Keep your eye on that lot," said Jack to his guards. "Looks like they'd shoot us down, given half a chance."

Louis Claude signalled the men to back off.

"Ignore them, Jack. Their sort have been fighting the English for the past hundred years under one Commander or another. Fighting is all they know. Let's get the cargo ashore, then we can be rid of them."

Jack's batmen stood either side of him, each holding a musket, while a motley collection of boats surrounded the luggers. Jack gave the signal to start unloading.

"Here, catch this, Frenchie," shouted Sam, throwing bales of the stinking wool over the gunnels. "I'm bloody glad to see the back of it. Give me your sweet kegs any day."

The laden boats set off for the shore, the chief French carrier keeping a tally as they were landed on the beach.

"By my calculation, Louis, you are now in possession of three tons of English wool," said Jack, as the last bale was unloaded. "According to the agent, Abe Mutter, payment will be in kind."

Louis nodded and signalled for the carriers to move the mules off the beach. Jack watched them leave with some relief. Their journey inland would not be easy. There was harsh competition between mill owners who were crying out for English wool, and the muleteers might be ambushed at any point along the narrow Normandy lanes.

"Yes, Jack, I am in agreement with that," said Louis Claude. He ordered the return cargo to be released and ferried aboard the waiting luggers.

No detail slipped past Jack. His batmen armed with pistols and swingle bats, stood guard around the boats. *An old friend Louis may be, but I'll take no chances*, he thought.

"I want this cargo well stowed, firm and steady, an' after it's loaded, make sure it's covered, with the oilcloth tied down tight. An' listen to this; at no time do I want more than half of the crew to be away from the boats, so work out who's goin' to eat first. There must be one armed guard on each boat. When you've finished loadin' and everythin' is shipshape you can go to the cottage at the back of the beach. It's got a laurel bush by the gate. There's a good feed laid on there, an' it's a safe house. We're leaving on the noon tide and you'll need you're wits about you, so don't go mad on the wine."

"Right, Louis, now that's organised we've got a couple of hours to catch up, but I want to stay in sight of the boats."

"Well I'm sure you want to eat and have a glass of wine with me, Jack. I'll send one of my men to bring us over some food." The two men walked along the shore to Louis' carriage, where they could sit in comfort and Jack could watch the loading, out of earshot of the crew.

"Well," said Louis, leaning back comfortably, "the last news I heard from Abe was that you were married with two children but that was before the war. Then a couple of years back I met up with a skipper from Lyme who said you were running a pub called the New Inn. Didn't sound like your line of business."

"You were right about that, the pub was a disaster," Jack smiled. "I feel as if I've lived a lifetime since we last met, some of it good an' some not so good. I'm thirty-four years old now, Louis, an' the last time we met I was just fourteen. I feel ashamed now to look back, but privateering sounded like the life for me at the time. We set off on a lugger called *Dover* making for the Azores. I thought I was set to make my fortune. But after a month at sea we was tricked by a French ship masquerading as an English brig. Just as we came alongside, the bastards ran up the French flag. We had no chance. She mounted twenty-six guns and we'd have bin blown out of the water."

Louis laughed. "I well remember the story, Jack. You cursed long and hard about it when they brought you into Bordeaux gaol."

Jack grinned, and marvelled again at Louis's easy use of the English language. "You taught me how to get around the women, Louis, it's always been useful, I've found. Let me see if I can remember. *Bonjour Madame, vous êtes tres belle aujourd'hui. Puis je vous aider avec votre sac?*" Jack repeated, in stumbling French, some of the phrases he had used to gain favour with the prison governor's wife, much to Louis' amusement.

"You may laugh, Louis, but it did the trick. I was allowed more liberties than the rest of 'em, an' after six months of tryin' it got me out of that poxy place." For the next hour Jack regaled his friend with the story of his escape from France on an American ship bound for New York. "It took another year to get home, but my God I had some stories to tell! The last two years in the pub has been another story and one best forgotten as far as I'm concerned. So now I'm back to free trading and maybe, Louis, we can do business together."

"Are you intending to work alone, Jack?"

"No, my son William is a strong lad, twelve years old an' rarin' to go. I'm bringin' him into the business. This war is causing a few difficulties moving goods, no doubt about that, but it can't last for ever, and when it's over there'll be good pickings, believe me."

40

Louis nodded. He had spent the last twenty years building up a small fortune from smuggling, but because of the war many of his friends and family were now either dead or in gaol.

"Keep in touch, Jack. I've some ideas you may well be interested in."

Jack could hear the sounds of revelry coming from the cottage, where an apparently endless supply of new wine was on tap.

"Better get the crew back on board before they get legless." He warmly shook hands with Louis Claude. "I'll be over before the year's out with a boat of my own," he said, and left to round up the crew.

Chapter 8

The men ran back to the beach in high spirits. A successful run put money in their pockets and food in their bellies. This was always cause for a celebration.

Jack could not believe his luck as he set the course for home. A brisk south-west wind took them out into the Channel and a steady drizzle set in, dropping visibility to twenty yards. Ideal conditions for a smuggling boat.

"If this keeps up we should be back in Beer Roads by 4 a.m. You keep watch, Tom, while I get my head down for a bit."

The trip was a real adventure for Tom. He sat on the prow listening to the waves slap the side of the boat and straining to see through the murk. Suddenly his young ears picked up voices.

"Mr Rattenbury, get up! I can hear somethin'."

Jack was awake in an instant. Not far off, he picked up the harsh voice of a captain giving orders to about face. "It's the Excise!" he shouted, and grabbed his musket. Two shots, the signal to scatter, warned the other two luggers, then, glancing at his compass, he turned the rudder fast to port, and headed towards Brixham. But, despite their best efforts, the cutter closed in fast.

"Jim an' Tom, get them kegs over the side. With a bit of luck we can pick 'em up tomorrow."

One by one sixty kegs were soon strung out behind the boat and swallowed into the rolling waves. Within twenty minutes the cutter came alongside.

"Heave to or I'll fire," shouted the Captain, but without waiting for Jack's response, set off a volley of small arms fire. Shot whistled through the air, smashing into the binnacle and bulwarks of the lugger. "You rascals, I'll put you all aboard a man-of-war." Captain Tingle, commanding HMS Catherine pulled alongside. "Search this boat from end to end, men. I know this man of old. He wouldn't be in mid-channel at this time of night an' not carrying contraband."

But the search proved fruitless. Captain Tingle sat in his cabin looking angry and disappointed. "Right, sir," he said formally, after inspecting the boat's log. "I intend detaining you and your craft. You will be taken to Brixham next week, but in the meantime you will accompany me while acting as convoy to the Brixham fishermen."

"What?" Jack spluttered with fury. "You have behaved towards me most shamefully. You have taken my vessel on the high seas and detained it, though you've found nothing aboard to justify doing so. I conceive this as an act of piracy."

The Captain listened, unmoved by the tirade. "That may be so, Mr Rattenbury – I believe that is your name – but in the meantime we shall proceed to Brixham where I shall go ashore for the night. You and your crew will remain on board under close supervision."

Abe and dozens of his men had been hiding on the beach for hours waiting for the luggers to come in. When he saw just two boats turn into Beer Roads, he knew at once that Jack was in trouble.

"Jack was always the first in," he thought, but with two luggers to get unloaded and the goods off the beach before first light he had to concentrate on the job in hand.

Hannah jumped when a sharp rap on the door woke her from a light doze in the early hours of Sunday morning. Thinking it was Jack she ran down to the kitchen and looked through the window. A dark face stared back.

"It's me, Mrs Rattenbury: Joe Stoker. I'm one of Jack's skippers."

Hannah opened the door. "Come in, come in Joe, you look all in. Get him some ale, Mother."

While Anne poured him a generous mugful, Hannah listened to Joe's tale.

"I got back into Beer an hour ago, Mrs Rattenbury, but we came across a cutter ten miles off Lyme Bay and Jack made off goin' west. He was tryin' to get em' off our course. The last I saw of him he was bein' chased towards Brixham but where he is now I don't know." Joe paused, "He may be all right, Mrs Rattenbury, but there was a lot of shootin'. He'd be bloody lucky to get out of that in one piece."

Hannah listened, her mind racing.

"You better get down the beach, girl," said Anne. "See if you can pick up any more news."

Hannah was already pulling on her cape and boots and stuffing her hair into a bonnet. "Thank you, Joe." I'll get down there an' see if I can find out where he might have ended up. Mother, you wake William, an' Frances will give you a hand with the baby." She ran down Fore Street, her cape flying.

"Hannah!" a familiar voice called from the darkness. Hannah was relieved to see Jane Bartlett running up Sea Hill towards her. "I've just heard from Stan Newton that they're aboard a cutter called the *Catherine* goin' into Brixham. He saw 'em way out in the bay and Jack shouted to him from the deck. I reckon we ought to get over there."

The two women ran on down to the beach where they found Abe. By now the luggers lay empty, the cargo on its way inland.

"Abe," Hannah shouted. "Stan Newton told us Jack an' the others is bein' held on the *Catherine* goin' into Brixham. Me and Jane are goin' over there on the coach to see if we can do anythin' to help".

"It'll take you days to get over there," said Abe, "an' who knows where they'll be by then."

But the women were not to be deterred. Hannah soon found a wet nurse in the village who, for a small sum, would take the baby while she was away. Within an hour arrangements had been made with Anne and she was ready to leave.

"If we get movin' now, Hannah," said Jane, "we can catch the morning coach up at Hangman's Stone."

However, while these feverish arrangements were being made Jack was a long way from Brixham.

Captain Tingle had received orders to provide protection for the fishing fleet from French privateers and the *Catherine* was heading for the Bay of Biscay along with fifty fishing smacks.

"We'll not be back for a week, gentlemen, so you can make yourselves handy," said Captain Tingle. He knew that he was bending the law by detaining Jack and his crew without evidence that they had been carrying contraband.

"I would like to point out, Captain Tingle," protested Jack, "that you have found no evidence upon which to convict me and therefore me and my crew are being held illegally."

The captain laughed. "Don't you worry about that, Mr Rattenbury. We've had our cutters out looking for kegs all night, 'round where we picked you up, an' no doubt they'll be found by the time we get back. Lock these men in the hold," the captain ordered the first mate. "I don't want to see them on deck till we're well out to sea. Rattenbury could fight his way out of a barrel, so I'm taking no chances with him."

Hannah and Jane arrived in Brixham exhausted and dishevelled.

"That's the last bloody time I'll be travellin' in any stinkin' coach," said Jane. "Nothin' but banging and clattering for mile on mile. My head feels like a bucket."

"Well, we're here now," said Hannah, "so stop your blathering and let's find out where the *Catherine*'s docked."

The harbour spread out below them as they walked down King Street. This was Jane and Hannah's first experience of such a large, busy port and they stared around in astonishment. A massive man-of-war lay at harbour bristling with guns, taking on fresh water and provisions. Hundreds of fishing smacks lined the quays alongside tall cargo ships off-loading goods from foreign lands. Hannah asked a woman selling fish where she could find out about the *Catherine*.

"Go an' have a word with the men by the wall. There's not much goes on in the harbour they don't know about."

Hannah tucked her hair back into her bonnet and pulled her shawl more tightly around her shoulders as she walked towards the men. Some had suffered devastating injuries in the war and were unable to work, others were fishermen too old to go to sea, and now spent their days fishing off the beach.

"I'm afraid you're out of luck, me lover," said a grizzled boatman sitting on the harbour wall. "The *Catherine* left two days ago for the Bay of Biscay. They won't be back for another five days."

Hannah looked at Jane in dismay. "Well, what now?" she said.

Jane thought quickly. "I've got some friends here, Josh Chapple and his wife, they used to live in Beer, but I haven't seen 'em in a long while. If they can't put us up I expect they'll know where we can get a cheap room."

Finding the Chapples was easier said than done. The two hungry, anxious women walked up and down the streets asking one person after another if they knew of a family by the name of Chapple. At last their luck changed. A young boy carrying a box of fish told them: "You'll find a family by that name down at the bottom of Middle Lane. I know they moved here a few years back from somewhere in Lyme Bay."

Jane knocked on the door of the cottage, quite expecting to be confronted with the face of a stranger, but when the door opened, Sally Chapple recognised her immediately.

"Come in, come in, Jane. What on earth are you doin' in Brixham?" She looked at Hannah curiously.

"This is Jack Rattenbury's wife," said Jane. "She came to the village after you'd left."

"Well, you both look as if you could do with a drop of somethin'. I'll get some bread and a bit of cheese on the table. Maybe you'll feel better with some food and a mug of ale inside you." The warm fug of the crowded cottage wrapped around Jane and Hannah like a blanket. Children stared at them in amazement from every corner.

Through the evening they related their tale of woe. The Chapples listened with much nodding and groans of sympathy. They had known Jack since he was a lad and were eager for news of Anne and their relatives in Beer. "Well, we can't offer you much but you're are welcome to stay here until they get back," said Sally, "as long as you don't mind squeezin' in with the children."

The next day the two women went back down to the dock to search for news. "I'm going to ask round an' see if they was spotted before they set sail," said Jane. She made her way along the harbour wall to where the men were sheltering from the wind.

"Yes, missus," said one, after a little persuasion, "The *Catherine* were holdin' prisoners, picked up for carryin' contraband, or so it was said."

"Did you get to speak to any of them?" asked Hannah.

"I know'd one of 'em was called Jack, an' he seemed to be getting the worst of the captain's tongue. Mind you, that Captain Tingle's a bit of a devil, better to keep out of his way, an' keep your trap shut. But this bloke Jack had a big mouth, an' he suffered for it. They came off once to get fresh water and dry provisions before they set sail."

The next few days were spent helping Sally in the cottage and wandering around Brixham marvelling at the sights. Each morning they walked to the top of Berry Head and after five days the *Catherine* came into view, just off Tor Bay. "That's her!" yelled Jane. "Come on!" They raced down to the harbour.

The two women watched expectantly as the cutter came in, shortly after the fishing fleet, and docked alongside the quay. They were buffeted by the press of sailors, eager to come ashore, and fishermen unloading their catch. After an hour or so they walked to the bottom of the gangway and, with some trepidation, asked to see Captain Tingle. His voice could be heard long before his bloated face appeared over the rail.

"What are you after?" he shouted. "Can't you see I've got work to do?"

"We know you are holdin' our men," said Hannah politely, "an' I would be most grateful if you would allow us aboard to see them."

"You've got a bloody cheek, woman, but as you've come so far you can have ten minutes."

With that he disappeared and could be heard ordering one of his men to bring up the prisoners. Jack, together with Jim, Tom and Sam were brought onto the deck. Jack had heard Hannah's voice and quickly constructed a desperate plan of escape, made from his observations of the crew's behaviour over the past week.

"Listen carefully, Hannah, we don't have long. As soon as you go ashore get hold of a good fishin' smack and come alongside tomorrow morning at six o'clock. The crew on this boat get bladdered out of their minds every night, an' Captain Tingle will be stayin ashore, so we might have a chance to get off."

"Right, time's up!" shouted the second mate and hurried the women towards the gangway.

"What do you reckon, Jane?" said Hannah as they walked out of the harbour. "Maybe Josh will help us get hold of a boat."

It didn't take long to persuade an ex-Beer fisherman to give his old friends assistance. "Don't you worry, I've got just the boat. If you can get clear of the harbour you might make it."

The next morning at precisely six o'clock Hannah and Jane rowed alongside the *Catherine*. A face looked over the rail and blinked in amazement. *I must be seein' things,* thought the gin-addled guard. *Two women in a boat. That bloody grog is picklin' my head.*

Hannah watched as Jack stole up behind the guard and hit him hard over the head with an empty bottle. His musket crashed to the floor, alerting the crew, but Jack and the others were over the rail and into the boat in seconds.

"Shove off, Hannah, an' keep rowing. I'll get the sail up," said Jack urgently.

The sound of feet pounding along the decks could be heard above them and sleep-drugged faces stared down at the small boat, now turning towards the harbour entrance.

"Stop or I'll fire," shouted the second mate. A round ripped straight through the sail, quickly followed by another, which split the halyard. The sail billowed into the bottom of the boat. Sam was knocked backwards and lay floundering under the rigging.

"Tom, get up that mast and reeve the halyard," Jack yelled. "We'll not let that bastard stop us."

Hannah and Jane continued to row valiantly, pouring every once of strength into keeping the boat moving.

"Don't want to give them an easy target," grunted Jane. "Thank God the tide's in our favour."

Jim and Sam pulled hard on the sail rope, resurrecting the damaged sail and the small craft responded readily.

"Ship the oars, girls," said Jack, roaring with laughter.

Despite the bullet holes, the wind caught the lugsail and sent the craft skimming out into the bay.

"You'll not get away with this, Rattenbury," shouted the guard, overcome with surprise, and fearful of the consequences. "We'll have you before the day's out."

But Jack was determined they would not be caught and with a mixture of courage and skill they managed to get clear of the harbour and reach Hope's Nose, a small promontory off Torquay.

"When we get on shore," said Jack, "take my advice, get inland as fast as you can."

The small boat hit the shingle with a crunch. Jack and Hannah scrambled up the cliffs, making for cover. Along the Brixham hills crowds of people had watched the escape, alerted by the musket shots. However, one sharp-eyed onlooker had spotted young Tom and Sam, hiding in a cave near the beach and promptly alerted the *Catherine*'s crew, who had launched a rowing boat and were closing in fast.

Jack and Hannah made good progress, keeping to small paths and farm tracks. It took them two days to reach Teignmouth, where they picked up a fishing boat going into Sidmouth. On arriving back in the village Jack made enquiries and found that Jane and Jim were safely home but Sam and Tom had been captured and were likely to be put aboard a man-of-war sailing for the West Indies.

Tom's mother was distraught. "First my husband, an' now my only son," she wailed." Jack stroked her head gently and held the sobbing woman in his arms. "Tom is like one o' my own," he said. "We can only pray that one day he'll return home unharmed."

Jack met up with Abe some days later. "Comin' across Tingle was bad luck, Jack, but as I told you, the buggers are everywhere these days and it's a miracle to get across without seein' an Excise cutter or privateers from both sides. Tom may be lucky an' survive, he's young enough, but I doubt poor old Sam will make it back to Beer. Life's bloody hard on them boats."

"Well, Tom's mother begged me to let him go, they're poor as church mice since his dad was taken."

"I'll give her what he would have earned on that trip," said Abe. "Apart from that disaster, the trip came off pretty well. To get two fully loaded boats back, packed to the gunnels with tea and kegs, is good for the pocket. I don't know yet if the kegs you chucked overboard were picked up. That would be a bonus." Abe paused. "We've got a good few trips lined up, so don't hang up your boots. I know you want to get that debt paid off, so the more runs you get in the better, Jack."

Chapter 9

Jack strode down Fore Street with a spring in his step and a smile on his lips for the first time in a long while. He was wearing a new jacket of heavy wool and knee-length leather boots, stout enough to keep his feet warm and dry. On the back of his head, worn at a jaunty angle was a sou'wester protecting him from the chill wind. The road was busy, full of carts laden with fish on their way to markets inland. Their heavy wooden wheels creaked and growled over the cobblestones. Jack knew most of the carters, who raised their hands to him. At the top of Sea Hill women sat swathed in shawls and surrounded by baskets of herring and blue-striped mackerel. Competition raged as to who could sell the most and shout the loudest.

"Five mackerel for half a penny, fresh off the boat."

Dealers stood on the beach, circling a large catch of skate, haggling fiercely over the price.

Jack called out to Jim Bartlett, just tying up the sale of a boatload of herring. "Got a good catch there, Jim."

His friend looked up, smiling broadly. "I've nearly finished here. How about meeting in the Dolphin for a jar?

"I'll be up there in an hour," said Jack. "Just goin' to look over the boat."

The retired fishermen hanging around Ponds Wall were eager to talk.

"How's it goin' Jack? Come over here a minute, out of the wind. Which way's this war going, do you reckon?" asked Isaac, bent and wizzened after a lifetime at sea.   "It's about time we saw the buggers off an' sent ol' Boney on his way."

"I'll give it another year," said Jack. "They still seem to have it in 'em for a fight, or at least that bloody warmonger Napoleon has. Most of the Frenchmen I come across would love to see the end of it."

"Well, it's knocking our trade, some families in this village are finding it hard to keep food on the table."

The day was cold, with a sharp wind coming in from the north. The men shivered and kept close in to the wall.

"We're keeping a look-out for the young Aplin lad," said Isaac. "He went out crabbing a while back, should be in by now."

As they spoke a shout went up from the beach and a small boat could be seen battling its way into Beer Roads. The heavy swell tossed the bows like a cork.

"Looks like he's made it, an' thank God for that," said Isaac. "Let's get down there, boys, and give him a hand." Whether paid or not, the men liked to help out on the beach and if all they got for it was a couple of mackerel, then so be it.

A year had passed since Jack had closed the New Inn and no opportunity for gainful employment had passed him by. *My God, I've been lucky,* he thought. The last instalment of his debt to Abe had been paid off six months ago and on the proceeds of his last trip Hannah had been able to fit the children out with some much-needed boots. Looking down on the beach, Jack watched as groups of small children, barefoot and frozen in the chill April morning, worked on the shore sorting fish. Jack knew how that felt and he could still hear the echo of the creed his mother lived by. "We'll never go on the parish, Jack. As long as there's fish comin' in we'll keep on workin, an' keep our heads up."

Mother and son formed a strong bond through those harsh years and despite Jack's undisputed love for Hannah, his mother remained a benign but strong influence. Jack had inherited her independence of spirit and could not countenance the thought of relying on others to determine his fate. Nothing had given him greater pleasure than handing over the last payment of the loan he had received from Abe. Now both men worked in close co-operation but Jack was once again master of his own destiny. He looked, with quiet satisfaction, at the *Volante* standing off shore. He'd struck a good bargain through Charlie Chapple but had never managed to discover the name of the other owner, either because Charlie didn't know his name or because he was reluctant to divulge it. Jack had bargained long and hard and smiled as he remembered the wrangling and push to get a good price.

"Well, you can tell whoever it is, Charlie, that if I'm to go ahead with it, I want the main say in how it's run," Jack had insisted. "Anythin' that earns money I'll take on, an' I hope that's understood. You can pass it back that I want fifty per cent of any income from whatever source, and let me know who the money's to be paid to."

No time had elapsed before Jack had got the reply he wanted and set out to drum up business. He now worked the *Volante* with William and by any standards they were doing well. Two trips to Alderney in the past week had been successful and, even taking part share, it was good money by anyone's book.

Hannah kept a careful eye on the boat's earnings and she reckoned that if Jack could achieve five successful runs in a month, then they would be doing well enough either to buy out the mystery partner or to purchase another boat.

"Changed your mind about smugglin', have you, Hannah?" said Jack lightly, after a particularly successful run.

"No, Jack, I have not," said Hannah sharply, and I want you to remember that each tradin' run should be followed by transporting legal cargo. That way we spread the risks and don't get too greedy. You're watched all the time in this village, but when the Excise don't know if it's legal or not, then it's easier to give 'em the run around."

Jack laughed. "You be a crafty minx."

"Well, let's hope our luck lasts, 'cause the money can be put to good use."

Jack paused and looked at Hannah, sensing a message. "What do you mean by that?"

"We've another on the way," said Hannah, "and soon this cottage is goin' to be at burstin' point. I've been thinking that we should build another, now that we have some extra money."

The news that another child was expected did not bring any reaction from Jack. It was viewed as an inevitable event.

"Well, I'm not movin out of this cottage," said Anne, taking them both by surprise. "You can do what you like, but this has been my home for all these years an' I'm not goin' anywhere."

"This place is near to fallin' down mother. There's a hole in the thatch and we can hardly swing a cat."

Anne looked at Jack, a deep frown creasing her forehead. "That's my last word on it." And with that she wrapped her shawl tightly around her shoulders and walked to the door. "I'm off down to see Mary Newton. If you want to come with me, John, you'd better hurry up."

Jack and Hannah looked at each other as the door closed with a firm thud. "You mark my words, Hannah, that's not the last word on it. We can't live here much longer, an' with another on the way it'll be near on impossible."

"She'll come round," said Hannah. "Anyway I've done some thinking. How about if we built a new place alongside this cottage, then we could repair the thatch for your mother an' she wouldn't have to move?"

William, who had been sitting silently throughout the discussion, pricked up his ears. "That would work, Father. Let's go an' measure up the plot before she gets back."

Jack found a long piece of twine to measure the ground-floor area and was soon looking over the long and narrow plot, pondering on possibilities. Anne's cottage stood against the rock face. It had been little more than a lean-to when first built, but over the years had been strengthened with extra timbers and constant patching of the cob walls.

"We've got a solid rock base to build on, Will. We could have two good-sized rooms upstairs over one large kitchen on the ground floor. That should give us a bit more elbow room."

After half an hour William and Jack returned, looking pleased with their efforts. "As far as I can see, Hannah, that should work just fine," said Jack expansively. "I'll put it to mother next week, when we get back from Cornwall."

William spent the following morning rigging the sloop in preparation for a trip to Newquay, leaving on the afternoon tide. He had spent the past six months working full time on his father's boat and had no regrets about leaving his apprenticeship at Chapple's. Jack was hard on him and that stung at times; he used his tongue very effectively to chastise his children and William had learnt to dread his father's inspections. Methodically he went over the standing and running rigging, checking every shackle and halyard. When his father hailed him from the shore for a lift in the tender he felt fairly confident that all was shipshape.

Jack climbed aboard, running his eyes over William's work. "What the bloody hell have you done there?" demanded Jack, looking in irritation at the foresail. "You should know by now to hank-on, starting at the tack of the sail."

William looked downcast and set about correcting his mistake, muttering under his breath and furious that his father had caught him out. Jack sat on the gunnels checking every inch of William's work. After a while he started whistling under his breath; William listened with relief knowing that everything else had passed muster.

Bloody ol' blimmer, he thought, and made up his mind not to give Jack the satisfaction of finding any more mistakes in future.

Jack looked out across the bay. White horses raced across Beer Roads. The sky was clear but early April could be changeable. "The wind's good and steady, Will, but it's goin' to be pretty lively by the looks of it, particularly round Land's End. You can get your head down for a while till we raise anchor, an' here's your grub." Jack handed William a lump of cheese with a hunk of bread and dripping sent down by Hannah.

"I'm going back ashore to have a pot of ale with Matt Westlake. The two Westlake boys are coming along with us. With the weather as it is we'll need all the help we can get on this one."

They were picking up a load of slate but, just as important for Jack, it gave him the opportunity to catch up with his contacts in Newquay and make sure he was known to any Link Man looking for a boat.

Chapter 10

Jack and William could be away for up to two weeks or more, depending on the weather. A severe storm could keep them in harbour for days at a time. Hannah was used to her husband's absences and had her work cut out caring for the children, of whom John was the most difficult. He idolised his father but while the latter was away John found himself in a house full of women. He was now nearly five years old and already known for fighting with boys on the beach and making a general nuisance of himself around the village.

"Eh! Johnny, we'll have 'ee bawlin 'yer' eyes out," taunted the local boys when passing him in the village. They knew how to rile him and enjoyed the spectacle of his face, red with fury, heading for another thrashing.

"You're running wild. Just wait till your father comes back!" Hannah would shout in frustration, giving John a smack around the ear, when, once again, he had reduced the baby or Frances to tears. At such times Anne would sniff with disapproval and her lips narrow, in an effort to hold back.

"Come here, me babby" she would coax quietly and slip him a treat from a small store concealed in her cupboard.

"You're spoiling that boy, Mother. He can wind you round his little finger," Hannah would snap. But she knew that without Anne's help, she would not be able to manage John at all.

John's other rival for Jack's attention was Frances. Whenever possible Jack would bring her small presents. A tiny cake of lavender soap was her favourite. It was wrapped in a small handkerchief, also a present from France, but never used. Frances knew that the slightest whiff of perfumed soap could arouse suspicions. Now just nine years old, she attended school for a few hours every day. The feud between Frances and her younger brother was bitter and ongoing. She loved her collection of special shaped pebbles found on the beach, some with holes worn through over the centuries, and pieces of driftwood smoothed and crafted by the sea. These treasures were kept in a small box and John could drive her into a fury by hiding it in the thatch.

"Where are my things, you scurvy little toad? Tell me now, or I'll lock you in the outhouse!" she would rail, pounding him with her fists. The threat of the outhouse gave John some pause for thought, but within ten minutes it was forgotten and once more he was preoccupied with finding ways to torment his sister. By the time Jack and William returned from their journeys, tensions were running high.

Hannah walked down to the beach to see Jack and William off on the noon tide. She had many friends in the village and her progress was slow as people stopped to ask after her health and how Jack was getting on. The gossip, following the visit from the bailiff, was now long forgotten. According to Anne, the whispers had moved on to a scandalous affair concerning the daughter of a fisherman who had taken up with a boy from Seaton.

In a group, the fishermen's wives were tough and formidable. They were used to spending days, if not months, alone while their husbands were at sea. Feuds and fights would often break out between them over trivial matters, but beware any outsider who interfered, or any of the authorities who would venture into the village seeking information. The women then stuck together like limpets and it would take a brave man to confront them.

"What you bin up to?" said Jane, eyeing her friend's bulging stomach. "You surely ain't carryin' agin?"

Hannah laughed. "Not far gone enough to stop me goin' out on watch with you tonight, Jane, if that's what you're worryin' about."

"I'm right glad to hear it, Hannah. Abe came to see me last week an' I said you would help me out. It's Harry Driver's boat, or so Abe told me. They be comin' in from Alderney round midnight."

"Give me a knock at 11.30 then, I'll be waitin' for you." Hannah hurried on down Sea Hill and could see the *Volante* standing offshore, rigged and ready to leave. "Hey, William!" she shouted, just making herself heard above the rattle of waves over the pebbles. "I've brought you some bread and cheese to take with you." She was rewarded by a warm smile from her son.

"Father's in the Dolphin, Mother. Give it to him to bring out," called William.

Abe Mutter was standing nearby engaged in tying up the final details of the run he had coming in from Alderney that night. He gave Hannah a wave. "You all right for tonight, Hannah?" he asked quietly.

Although Hannah was reluctant to admit it, she was grateful for the help he had generously given Jack. "That I am, Abe. I've just bin' talkin' to Jane and we'll be there at midnight."

Hannah looked around the beach and, like Jack, knew every person working there. She both loved and hated the village. It could feel claustrophobic and cut off from the rest of the world.

It was different in Lyme, the atmosphere was different, she thought. *Plenty of tradin' goin' on but the port brought in people from all over and we were used to seeing strangers about the place. But since I moved here, it's as if my other life ceased to exist. Jack comes and goes but the village is my whole life.* She turned and made her way across the beach. *Ah well,* she thought, *nothin' to worry about on this run. No excise cutter will be interested in a cargo of slate and, God willin', they'll be safely back in Beer by the end of next week. I'll get some dabs for tea and get back home for a rest.*

"You all right, me lover?" Jack bellowed, when he spotted his wife pushing her way through the throng of fishermen and traders around the bar. He planted a wet enthusiastic kiss on her cheek.

Hannah handed over the bread and cheese wrapped in a cloth. She could see that Jack was well in his cups and overflowing with bonhomie.

"You need to get down to that boat or you'll miss the tide," she said sharply. "I'm off home."

"Right you are, woman. Take care of yourself tonight, Hannah," he whispered and, giving her a mock salute, turned to his friend with a wink. "Looks like I've got to be off now, Jim, the lads is waitin' aboard and we'll need to get movin' if we want to get into Newquay before Thursday marnin'."

"Well, keep me in mind for anythin' that comes up, Jack. We could always do with a bit extra."

"That I will, Jim, your lads is growin' fast, an' they be mighty useful on a boat. I'll see what I can do for you."

William was relieved to see his father making his way unsteadily down Sea Hill and set off in the tender to bring him aboard. "You've had a few by the looks of you, father," said William, laughing at Jack staggering over the shingle, and swiftly took possession of the food before it dropped overboard.

To anyone watching, the couple made a comical pair, crammed into the tiny tender, Jack throwing his arms about, laughing loudly and hailing anyone within earshot. At last, William pulled his father aboard and, feeling the deck beneath his feet, Jack sobered.

"Nothin' to worry about on this run, Will, it's all above board. The excise cutters can chase us all they like; I fancy giving them a run for their money." Jack threw his jacket down into the cabin and flexed his shoulder muscles. "Come on, me lads, weigh anchor an' haul on the sheets."

The sails filled with a sharp snap, sending the craft ploughing through the waves and out into Beer Roads. The two Westlake boys kept the sails trimmed, close-hauled and on port tack. "You're doing well there, boys," shouted Jack. "If we keep this southerly wind we'll make good time."

These days Jack confided in his son on a man-to-man basis. William had a good head on his shoulders. "At this rate, Will, we should get in by Thursday marnin'. We'll load the slate as fast as we can, then I want to get round the pubs to see who's about. We could do with another run over to Cherbourg but it's got to be with an honest broker, I didn't get my fair cut on that last run."

Will nodded his head. He was aware of the danger of taking up with unreliable agents and there were always plenty hanging around the ports on the look-out for a likely skipper.

"I want to come out on the next run, Father. I know enough now, an' I could do a good job."

"I know that well enough, son, but there's more to it than handlin' a boat. When you've seen the inside of a gaol, as I have on too many occasions, you'll know what I'm talkin' about."

William listened to his father impatiently and, with the ignorance of youth, remained convinced that he would never fail to outwit the patrolling excise cutters. "Just take me on one run and I'll show you," he wheedled.

"Be patient, William, when the time's right I shall be grateful for your help, an' take my word, it's not far off."

The week wore on, each crew member taking their turn at the helm, as the craft made its way down the coast, heading for Land's End before turning into the heavy swell of the Atlantic.

Hannah was waiting when a light tap on the door came at 11.30. "I'm off now, Mother, let's hope it's a quiet night," she said.

She and Jane slipped up the back lanes onto the Common, well wrapped up in wool capes and bonnets. The night was black as pitch but both knew every rut. Their eyes scanned the dips and gulleys, watching for a shift in the shadows, listening for a muffled footfall. But all was silent and deserted. At last, they reached Beer Head and dropped down into a small hollow on the edge of the cliffs surrounded by low scrub. The night closed around them, their bodies merged with the bushes into the blackness.

"We should be able to see 'em in the next half-hour, Hannah. The boat's due into Beer Roads around midnight but it looks like the wind's droppin' a bit, that might slow 'em down."

Below them the roar of the waves pounding on the rocks could mask the creek of a harness or the snort of a restless horse, standing for hours, in the darkness. Jane placed her hands flat on the hard ground. Sometimes the vibrations of horses hooves could be felt, pounding over the path from Branscombe. "It's bloody freezin'! Let's hope they get here soon," she muttered.

Hannah held the spout lantern tightly in her hand; at the first hint of a Riding Officer in the vicinity, she would briefly flash the light and scupper the landing. Needless to say, this was not done lightly. As soon as any skipper saw the light, kegs would be thrown overboard and maybe lost. From then on the smugglers' lives were at risk while they desperately hauled up the sails and made for the open sea.

"There they be!" whispered Jane. She had spotted the dim outline of a lugger making its way towards Hooken beach. The women stared into the darkness, examining the cliff path inch by inch, alert to any sign of movement.

At last two boats were pushed off into the pounding waves to pick up the contraband. Icy-cold sea water crashed into the gunnels, drenching the crew, who rowed frantically towards the waiting lugger.

"Hurry up an' get this lot ashore!" shouted Abe, counting steadily as the kegs were piled into the bilges. At last, the laden boats cast off and made for the beach where the carriers were waiting in the shadows. Within thirty minutes the goods were away into the lanes.

"Come on, Hannah, let's get goin', I'm frozen to the bone," said Jane. "Abe will pay us down on the beach tomorrow."

Jack was confident that Hannah could keep her nerve while keeping watch and would have no better companion than Jane, but there was always the danger of being discovered. The penalties for assisting in a smuggling run were severe indeed and could lead to a lengthy prison sentence or worse.

Anne sat up waiting for Hannah to get in and offered her a drink of brandy and warm water. She would never have admitted it but the hours were long while she waited for her daughter-in-law to return. "Soon thaw you out, girl," she said, when Hannah slipped the latch on the door and drew her chair up close to the fire.

Hannah often found it difficult to sleep after returning from 'a watch' and was happy to sit with Anne and talk things over. "I saw Mary, Tom's mother, today," said Anne. "She was pleased you had found some news of him."

Hannah had written to The Admiralty in London, soon after Tom was captured in Brixham. She had been given the name of his ship and, as there was no mention of his death, it was assumed that he was still 'serving His Majesty'.

"At least he's still alive," said Mary, when Hannah relayed this good news. "That's somethin' to be thankful for. Not like his poor father."

"I asked if she would come round an' help with the babby in the morning," said Hannah. "She's grateful for the help we give her, but a proud woman like that finds it difficult, an' always needs to let you know it."

Anne nodded her head and parroted Mary's words. "'I don't like taking charity, Mrs Rattenbury, but I'm willing to work when there's a need. Let's hope our Tom gets back fit and well, then we can hold our heads up.' I tell her not to worry, I know what it feels like to be constantly lookin' for enough food to put on the table. We've all had it one way or t'other."

Hannah nodded in agreement. "Well, I know that Jack feels bad about what's happened to Tom. Let's hope the boy gets back to Beer and none the worse for wear. Now I'm for bed, Mother," she said, rubbing her eyes, and made her way up the narrow stairs.

Chapter 11

William watched his father at the helm, holding a steady course as the sloop pitched and rolled in the heavy seas off Land's End. It was a lively trip all right with all hands on deck and by the time they came in sight of Newquay they were all aching for a good meal and a rest.

The quays were bustling with life and the fishing fleet were preparing to leave as the sloop pulled alongside. Up to a hundred boats lined the harbour wall. Men were checking rigging and loading nets. Jack searched among the clerks, bustling around the quays, and was directed to his cargo of slate, waiting in carts alongside the sea wall. "You stay round here while this slate's loaded, William, an' get the boat rigged for the trip back. Here's a shillin' to get you and the lads a pasty an' a mug of ale. I'm goin' off round the pubs."

Sitting quietly in the snug of the George and Dragon, Jack watched the customers come and go. Newquay attracted sailors from far and wide, looking to find work around the busy port, but the agents were a different breed. They looked more prosperous, not ostentatiously so, but there was something about them that spoke of confidence and money. Jack listened carefully as the pub talk flowed around him, giving voice to the usual concerns of men whose livelihood depended on the weather and the ups and downs of trading. Suddenly a hand settled lightly on his shoulder. Jack stiffened as a soft voice whispered, "Ça va, Monsieur Rattenbury?"

Jack didn't need to look around. "Louis, just the man I'm relief. "What brings you to Newquay?"

The two men had not met since Jack had returned from the trip to Cap la Hague twelve months previously and Louis was curious to know how Jack had fared on the trip and how his plans for business were working out.

"I don't know if you ever heard what happened, Louis, but that trip was a hot one. It was a profitable trip, I'll give

64

you that, but we lost one boat and its load of kegs. I had a lucky escape from an excise cutter with the help of my wife, but that's another story. Sadly, two of my crew were captured and are now somewhere in the Caribbean servin' on a man-o'-war."

Louis listened avidly. "There's no doubt in my mind, Jack, that the sailors who get the goods across the water are in a class of their own. I have to leave such things to younger men, like you," he sighed, somewhat unconvincingly.

Louis was now well into middle age. His subtly cut expensive clothes skilfully disguised his portly figure, acquired during a lifetime as a bon viveur. He loved all the good things France had to offer, despite the endless wars engaged in by Napoleon: fine wines, haute cuisine, and a rich life filled with culture and leisure. He was born into a family with aristocratic connections, a true gentleman of the upper classes. However, on closer inspection it was apparent that Louis liked to dip in and out of this charmed life and took great pleasure in earning large amounts of money through dabbling in the smuggling trade. His meeting with Jack in the Bordeaux gaol had been his one and only brush with the law and since that time he had taken great pains to conceal his nefarious activities. When meeting him for the first time at the age of fourteen, these anomalies had gone over Jack's head, but since then he had had time for reflection.

"Since getting out of the pub things have gone well for me, Louis. I've decided to buy another boat when I get back from this trip. Got my eyes on a twenty-oared galley that's up for sale in Lyme, a very useful craft for moving goods, as you know."

"A wry smile flickered around Louis' lips. "That's what I like to see, enterprise. I could see it in you at just fourteen years of age."

Jack silently registered this compliment. "I've also got part share in a lugger, which is doing well, an' that's what I'm doin' here, Louis, looking for a good run. Any ideas?"

Louis looked thoughtful. "I've just taken delivery of a stock of kegs which are to be stored in Alderney. Sounds like just the thing you're looking for."

The two men ordered a light meal and sat for the next hour working out tide schedules, quality of goods and profit margins.

At last Jack sat back, feeling pleased with himself. He enjoyed driving a hard bargain. "We'll shake hands on that one, Louis, and let me buy you a drink," Jack waved expansively for a bottle of good French brandy. "Now tell me, my friend, what are you doing in Newquay? England is a risky place for a Frenchman to find himself in these days."

Louis smiled enigmatically. "I have many strings to my bow, Jack, but take it from me, I am not unwelcome in your country."

By the time Jack had finished tying up the details of the run with Louis, he had drunk his fill and was in no condition to question the Frenchman on this veiled remark. "Time I went, Louis. The boy will be waiting to cast off. Don't want to miss the evenin' tide."

William watched his father winding his way back along the quay and put out a hand to help him aboard.

"Come on, Father, we need to get off," he shouted into his ear. Within ten minutes Jack had his head down on a pile of nets and was sleeping soundly.

The Frenchman turned out to be the good trading contact Jack had needed and for the first time in many years he could look forward to expanding his activities. His plan to purchase another boat, winsomely called *Friendship,* was achieved; many lucrative runs were made with this craft during spring and summer between Beer and Alderney. Now, well into October, the autumn mists were back and of no great hindrance to those who would slip in and out of tucked-away coves without attracting attention.

Louis, Jack observed, made sure to stay in the background while carrying out their negotiations, but after working closely with Jack for ten months or more, he sent word suggesting a meeting. Hannah read the letter carefully. "It's about some deal, Jack. He says to meet him in Omonville first week in November. He's keeping a low profile for the time being, and wants no one to know of his whereabouts. Said he'd pay you well, two hundred guineas."

This sum was far in excess of the profit made on an average run but Jack knew better than to question his friend, whom he trusted implicitly. *Must be risky for that amount of money*, Jack pondered, *but I'll not quibble on it and maybe this is the time for William to come along.*

Jack gave William the benefit of all the information he had about the trip but had to acknowledge that he was in the dark himself as to what would be required of them. "All I know for sure, Will, is that we'll need to get in and out quickly and without bein' spotted. This time we won't be carryin' anythin', so there's no danger of bein' picked up by the excise but the Frenchies is always on the look-out for seamen to crew their men-o'-war, an' that's the last place we wants to end up."

William could hardly contain his excitement. He had waited over a year for this and although it wasn't a true contraband run, it had all the elements of danger that he lusted after.

"Think it's best you keep this trip to yourself, Will. If anybody wants to know where we're goin', just say we're off down round Falmouth looking to buy another boat."

According to plan they set off, catching the noon tide, and apparently heading for the south-west out of Lyme Bay. Jack had decided to put into Exmouth for the night and head for the Cherbourg peninsula the following morning. They left before dawn. The sloop felt easy and responsive. It was a novelty for William and his father to be out alone on the open sea, battling to wring every ounce of power from the wind and with no danger of being picked up by the excise.

"I've got to give it to you, Will, you're a bloody good sailor – nearly as good as your father," Jack laughed. Salt spray whipped his face until his skin was red raw.

William grunted and looked quickly away, watching for every advantage. *I'll bloody show him one of these days,* thought William.

The night was black as pitch when they finally turned into the bay. Jack peered over the side of the boat examining the plumb line. "Haul the sail down, Will," Jack whispered. "We'll use the oars for the last half-mile." He was on tenterhooks.

The coast was crawling with militia based in a small fort which stood within a mile of the shore. Neither father nor son spoke a word as the boat slid towards the shallow beach. At last, with a gentle whish, they came ashore and William dropped over the side to pull the boat up onto the sandy beach. A small cove, edged with a rock outcrop, concealed them from the customs house and, more importantly, from any French or British man-o'-war cruising the coast.

"Remember!" Jack whispered as he left. "Keep silent and stay in the boat. If you're spotted leave without me; I'll get back somehow." He made his way up the beach to find Louis waiting in the shadow of the rocks. They swiftly made their way to a nearby safe house.

"Well, my friend, it's good to see you again. I've no doubt you are curious as to why I've brought you here."

Jack waited and sat forward on the wooden bench, watching the Frenchman closely.

Louis sighed. He looked haggard and weary; a far cry from the light-hearted man Jack was used to meeting. "This war seems endless, Jack. So many of my family and friends have died or are imprisoned in English gaols."

Jack was taken by surprise, rarely had he seen Louis so despondent. He sat quietly, aware that his friend was struggling to find words for his distress. The silence lengthened and at last Jack spoke. "You know, Louis, most of my business is with the French, I want the situation to settle down and no more lives to be lost but I live mostly outside the law of my country, so it's hard to be a patriot, particularly in these times. If truth be known, I feel so strongly against the Government's policy of impressing innocent and hard-working seamen that my political views are entirely flexible, and likewise my loyalties. I do whatever keeps me in work and provides for my family."

Louis looked relieved. "I'll be frank with you, Jack, I have a brother in Tiverton gaol. He was serving on a man-o'-war before being captured with three other officers, that was two years ago. He is desperate to get back to France and see his family and I'm looking for a way to get him out of England."

Jack had heard of many such transactions over the years. Tiverton held a large number of French prisoners. Most were of good social standing and frequently allowed out on parole but, until this time, he had had no idea that the gaol held any of Louis' family.

"Louis, you must know that an arrangement like this will be costly. Gaolers will have to be paid off and I would need to find somewhere safe to hide the men along the coast before getting them aboard."

Louis nodded vigorously and held up his hand. "The money is of little importance, Jack. I have thought this matter over for a long while and I am prepared to be generous. I already have many contacts in Tiverton, so leave the other arrangements concerning the gaolers to me. I will send word when and where you have to pick them up and it's likely you will need to hire horses. As I said in the letter, Jack, I will pay you two hundred guineas."

Jack barely hesitated. During the past two years a small contingent of Dragoons had been stationed in Beer and contributed greatly to the hazards suffered by smugglers.

"Is that all, Louis?"

"Not quite, Jack. This letter, I need it delivered to Sir William Pole urgently. I believe you know of him. Before this damned war started we were in regular contact and he remains a loyal friend. He has promised to help me in some other matters but needs the information contained in this missive. You will have to take my word that I have done all I can to ensure that you are not implicated in any way."

They shook hands and Louis kissed Jack on both cheeks in the French manner.

No two men could be more disparate but mutual respect bound them, and the knowledge that they were equally of benefit to each other.

The meeting had taken just short of an hour but for William, waiting silently in the boat, it had seemed double the time. His relief was palpable when Jack swung over the side of the boat.

"Let's get out of here quick, Will, a bit too hot for my liking."

The boat slipped off the gently sloping beach with barely a ripple giving notice of its presence and as the sails filled, the craft surged forward into the swell, picking up a fresh south-westerly breeze and was soon out into the Channel. "Well done, Will, that was a grand bit of work. There's nothing to worry the excise men on this boat, so let's get back home quick."

Jack stuffed the letter into his shirt. *No excise man will be looking for anything other than a few kegs on a boat this size,* he thought, and reflected on the conversation with Louis. *It's going to be bloody difficult to hide four grown men in Beer, particularly with the place packed with the military.*

It took just over twelve hours before Jack and William came in sight of Portland on the starboard bow. William was shivering with cold and fatigue. "What was all that about, Father?" he'd asked several times during the night, but Jack was not to be drawn.

"You'll have to wait, Will, it's a bit outside our usual line of business. When it's over I'll tell you about it. In the meantime, keep your mouth shut. I don't want your mother diggin' round, so just tell her you sat in the boat while I talked over a run with Louis." He was certain Hannah would consider the whole escapade far too risky, in a different league altogether from the usual business of running contraband.

Arriving back at the cottage, William and Jack sat down to a good breakfast and it quickly became clear that keeping Hannah in the dark would not be easy.

"And how was Monsieur Claude?" she asked, when it became apparent that neither Jack nor William was forthcoming with any information.

Jack chewed on his bread and meat, feeling uneasy. "He sends you his regards, Hannah, and hopes we can all meet up when this war's over. Didn't seem like his normal self this time, the war's gettin' him down. Several of his family have been killed."

With that bit of information Jack hoped she would be satisfied and quickly diverted the talk into instructing William to swab down the boat and prepare the rigging for the next day. Hannah looked long and hard at Jack. She knew intuitively that there was more to it but decided to let it go for the time being.

"I'll give you a hand with the boat, William," she said.

Jack signalled William to keep his mouth shut.

Chapter 12

Jack had made up his mind to get the letter to Sir William that day. Louis had given him no clue as to its content, which, in accordance with their association, was unusual. Now, standing in the safety of his own home, Jack held the letter between his fingers and considered prizing open the seal.

"What's that?" asked Anne, who had just returned from fetching the water.

"It's a letter to be delivered to Sir William Pole," said Jack, "an' I would dearly like to know what it contains."

"You better get that over to Sir William an' out of your hands quick, Jack, 'cause it sounds to me like it could mean trouble if it was found in this cottage. There's more to that Louis Claude than you realise, in my opinion. Men like him don't like to get their hands dirty, but lets others do it for 'em."

"I think you're right, Mother," said Jack. "Tell Hannah when she gets back that I'll be away for a night, maybe more. I'm goin' on over to Tiverton when I've delivered the letter."

Anne looked at Jack curiously. "Tiverton? What you doin' goin' over there?" But she could see by the look on his face that she wouldn't get any more information out of him.

Jack concealed the letter in his shirt and made his way up through the village to the stables. He planned to hire a horse for a couple of days with the intention of riding on to Tiverton after delivering the letter. He could then check the best route back to Beer through the back lanes. Jack would never have described himself as an expert horseman but he could manage a steady plod, which was all the old mare was up to. He felt weary after the trip to see Louis and as he made his way up through the lanes towards Colyton he was grateful to let the horse do the work and give his body a well-earned rest. The gentle ride also gave Jack time to think, and the more he thought about Louis' proposal, the more uneasy he became. *This could be a hangin' offence, an' a bloody site more risky than handlin' a boat load of kegs.* Alarming ruminations bounced around his agitated mind, with little to distract him, other than the occasional rabbit, which gave the mare a fright and sent her skittering sideways into the hedge.

Shute House stood in lonely splendour amid rolling green fields. Dotted here and there were small thatched farm cottages. Jack had never before visited the house and had passed it only once in his life when on the road to Tiverton, as a boy.

As he rode up the well-tended drive, a guard, dressed smartly in a leather tunic, stepped out of the gatehouse and demanded to know his business. The imposing entrance, built in Tudor times, bore the Pole coat of arms, in pride of place over the entrance. The motto *Pollet virtus*, 'Virtue excels', would no doubt have amused Jack, had he been able to read it.

"My name is Jack Rattenbury an' I've a private letter for Sir William sent to him by a close friend, I have orders that it should be given to him in person."

The guard looked at Jack suspiciously. He had taken care to smarten himself up a bit but he could in no way pass as a gentleman, and the old mare, standing with her head drooping with fatigue, was further proof of his lack of social standing. "Tie your nag up here," said the guard, barely concealing a smirk, "and I'll get someone from the house to come down and get you."

A servant came down to collect Jack and on the way up to the house he questioned her closely as to Sir William's disposition and what reception he could expect.

"You've nothin' to worry about with him," said the girl. "He's a perfect gentleman and treats us all well, very generous indeed."

Jack was shown into a sumptuously ornate hall by a footman who asked his name and what business he had with Sir William.

"You can tell Sir William," said Jack loudly, "that I have an important letter from his friend Monsieur Louis Claude and I've bin requested to deliver it to himself in person."

The footman ran his eyes over Jack's rough clothing in an attempt to intimidate. Jack stared back, a cocky lift of his chin sending out an indisputable message.

Left alone in the hall, Jack had time to look around. Never in his life had he seen anything so magnificent. Ancient tapestries hung on the walls alongside oil paintings of the Pole family, going back generations.

"Ah, Rattenbury, is it?" Sir William had walked quietly up to Jack without being noticed, lost as he was in examining his surroundings.

Jack started slightly, "That's my name, Sir William."

"Well my man, I believe you have a letter for me."

Jack pulled the letter out of his shirt and handed it over with some relief. "From our mutual friend Monsieur Louis Claude," Jack declared with a show of bravado.

Sir William smiled, somewhat amused at Jack's cheek and accepted the letter. "No doubt I'll be seeing you again, Mr Rattenbury," and, pressing a guinea into Jack's hand, said, "Will you please accept this small recompense for your trouble."

Jack left Shute House feeling none the wiser as to what Sir William's connection with Louis Claude might be, but he was somehow sure that this man had some unspecified connection with his own life.

Jack rode on into Tiverton, taking careful note of side lanes and cart tracks which could be used by travellers wishing to keep off the main highway. He entered the town during early evening and promptly found a bed in a local inn. After making arrangements for stabling the horse, he set off around the town and was interested to note that the lanes were full of French men and women mingling easily with the local inhabitants. He took a seat in a small public house and made it his business to open up a conversation with the publican. "What's all these Frenchies doin' wanderin' around the town?" he asked.

The publican laughed. "I'm not complaining about it, sir, as they bring me in good business but they is prisoners of war. Every day they is let out of gaol but when the curfew bell rings in St George's Church they have to return without delay. Not allowed more than a mile from the gaol, or so I'm told."

"Well, I'm damned!" said Jack. "I'd have thought they'd have tried to get back to their own country. Can't be much fun stuck here in that godforsaken gaol."

"It has been known to 'appen sir, two of 'em legged it when the curfew bell rang last year, but not as many clear off as you might think. I reckon life ain't that rosy in La Belle France."

Jack bade him goodnight and wandered off around the town. Most of the prisoners looked well fed and although their clothes were worn and frayed, they had been of the highest quality. He took note that when the curfew bell rang, they turned and, without any show of reluctance, walked back towards the gaol.

Once more Jack's thoughts turned to the problems associated with transporting a live cargo. *Louis will have arranged for them to escape during the day and they'll be hidden until after dark, but that's not my problem. If Louis is going to spring four prisoners I'll have to work out where to hide the buggers until the time's right to make a swift trip over the water. What I've got to do is find a place on the way back to Beer where I can wait for them without being seen. Just below Shute House on the edge of Sir William's land would be out of the way. I'll take a look on the way back tomorrow.*

Jack didn't sleep soundly that night. He couldn't put his finger on why but he had an uneasy feeling about the run. Back and forth his mind ranged over the possible pitfalls. *Kegs are quiet and don't need feedin'. How in hell's name am I going to get them onto a boat without someone raising the alarm?* But by the time daylight filtered through the narrow window of the inn a rough plan had formed in his mind. *I'll start from the beginning. First off, I'll time the ride back to Beer,* he thought, and left Tiverton as the sun climbed over the hills to the east. Just past Shute he noted a small copse where he could meet up with the prisoners and their guides; it had taken him just over four hours to reach this spot and the sun was now high in the sky. By Jack's calculations it should be around noon. He sat back in the saddle and tried to ease his aching backside. *This might just work out,* he thought. *Think I'll hole them up in the quarries to start with. That way I can get in a store of food beforehand and only move them down into the village when I've got the boat ready and the tide and wind is right.*

By the time Jack rode down Bovey Lane into the village he was feeling more positive.

"Well, are you goin' to tell us what's goin' on Jack?" asked Hannah as soon as he came through the door. "Your mother told me you've delivered a letter to Sir William Pole, an' then went on to Tiverton." Hannah waited expectantly.

"You can jabber on as much as you like, woman, but you'll get nowhere. I want some vittles now," said Jack, and banged his fist down hard on the table. "An' where's our Will?"

Jack felt tired, hungry and agitated. The last thing he wanted was a long interrogation from Hannah. After eating a good meal of fat bacon and eggs he fell into a deep sleep, greatly helped by a few pots of ale and a generous tot of brandy.

But Hannah and Anne were put out by his rough rejection. The atmosphere in the cottage became charged. Hannah quizzed William continually behind Jack's back, trying to find out the cause of his unease, but William was no wiser than his mother and could not shed any light on the matter.

"I reckon it's got somethin' to do with that Louis Claude," said Anne. "He's not bin the same since that trip with our William."

Hannah could only wait and speculate.

After waiting a week and with much soul searching, Jack decided to send Louis a small map, indicating the copse where he could meet up with the prisoners and suggesting that it would take just over four hours by horseback from Tiverton.

He racked his brains on how this could be done without arousing suspicion. *It's no damn good*, he thought. *I'll just have to get our Will to help me.*

William had kept clear of his father since their trip to France but the boy had a lively brain and constantly turned over events in his mind, looking to find a reason for the change in his father's light-hearted nature. So he was surprised one morning when Jack suggested they take a walk up over the Common. When they were well away from the busy path, Jack turned to his son and placed a hand on his shoulder. "This might come as a bit of a shock, Will, but I need your help."

William tensed, not knowing what to expect.

"That trip to France, Will," Jack took a deep breath and said, in a rush, "it's about smuggling some French prisoners from Tiverton gaol over to Cherbourg."

William looked at his father in horror. "You must have gone soft in the 'ead, father. Gran's right, that Louis Claude's behind this."

"Just listen. Louis is payin' me two hundred guineas. I can't turn down that sort of money."

"Well, what is it you want me to do?" asked William.

"I want you to write out these directions showing the route from Tiverton to Shute crossroads, where I'm goin' to pick up the prisoners. You know I can't do writin'."

William sat down on a log looking apprehensive, but slowly he warmed to the idea. The sum of two hundred guineas was a small fortune and his mind leapt with excitement at the thought of such a sum. "Right, Father, I'm up for it, but where can we get this map done without mother findin' out?"

The following week Joe Stoker was leaving on another trip to Alderney and going with him, concealed in a clay pipe, was a rough map and written instructions showing the route from Tiverton to the copse near Shute House.

Chapter 13

Months went by without Jack receiving further instructions, but one night, as the family were settling down for bed, a light knock sounded at the front door. Jack answered it to find Joe Stoker holding a scrap of parchment. "Brought this for you, Jack, from your friend in Alderney."

Jack stood looking at the parchment; a feeling of dread crept up his legs and settled lightly around his throat. "Thanks, Joe," he whispered. "I'll make sure you get somethin' for bringin' this over."

Joe was an excellent seaman, but well known for his complete lack of interest in anything other than catching sea bass and growing potatoes. A message, which would have had many others scratching their heads, left Joe without a trace of curiosity. "All right, Jack?" he would chirp brightly, after delivering a missive, which could be anything from a string of figures to a meaningless few words. "I'm off now, down the beach, out with Greg, tryin' to catch a bass."

Jack shut the door firmly and sat down to look at Louis' instructions. *Bloody hell*, he thought, trying to decipher the scrawled words, *I'll have to get our William to have a look at it.*

"What was all that about?" said Hannah, when Jack climbed back into bed.

"Nothin'," Jack grunted and turned his back.

The next morning Jack and William went for another walk over the Common.

"What do you make of this, Will? Joe brought it round last night when you was out fishin'."

"Twenty days after Sunday – at midnight," said William, stumbling over the unfamiliar letters. He stared at his father, sickening thoughts racing through his mind.

"Well, I'm stuck with it now, William. As you know, Louis has been a good friend of mine for many a year. Without him you and your mother would have known hard and bitter times. He's kept me in tradin' for the last twelve months, an' kept a sharp eye out for my livelihood. What harm's it goin' to do to get four men back to their homeland? Anyway, William, I decided as soon as Louis put it to me, that you would not be involved in the actual run. If somethin' should 'appen, your mother's goin' to need you, but I do want you to give me a hand gettin' some stores up to the quarries. That's where I'm goin' to hide 'em until the wind an' tide's right."

The tension in the cottage became worse. Jack's temper was short and even Frances could not make him laugh. Hannah noticed that William and his father were constantly disappearing and holding whispered conversations.

"What are you two cooking up?" said Anne one morning, when catching Jack and William coming through the gate just before dawn.

"Keep your nose out of things, Mother," Jack snapped, and pushed past her into the kitchen. Hannah looked up when Jack barged through the door; she had given up trying to find out what was going on and relations between them had become strained and distant.

The weeks crawled past. Jack and William continued to busy themselves in fishing around the cove and short trips delivering cargo, but all the while plotting, planning and waiting. Jack had given much thought to preparing the cavern as a hiding place for the Frenchmen, and thick woollen blankets and oilskins were now well hidden under piles of bracken. William eventually overcame his horror of the place and was soon used to slipping away up the dark lanes taking with him baskets of cheese, ale and a good supply of candles. Both father and son struggled with the fear of being caught and betrayed, but neither spoke of it.

In a sudden quickening of events, the night was upon them. Jack left the village during the course of the afternoon and took a circuitous route around Seaton in order to allay suspicion. He reached Colyford by early evening and stopped at an inn by the River Axe for a sup of ale. Sitting on the bank, he stared at the soft flow of fresh water, the gentle undulating reeds lulled him away from the thoughts which had held his mind in an icy grip for the past months. All around were signs of late summer. The fields held sheaves of freshly cut, honey-perfumed hay, drying in the sun. With regret, Jack left this restful place and walked on up through the hills to Whitwell, where he hired five horses from some stables. As each of his careful plans was accomplished Jack ticked them off in his mind. The stable hand did not question Jack's request for five horses, to be returned before dawn, but saddled them up and handed Jack the reins. *Can see he's not bin round hosses much,* he thought.

Jack made his way to the copse feeling awkward and out of his element. After tying up the horses securely, he lay down to rest and eat the bread and cheese Anne had put together for him. Noisy rooks circled as the shadows lengthened, and silently, the night closed in. The moon was on the wane but the night was bright enough to be worrying and Jack looked out from his hiding place at the lanes snaking down through the valley, etched in starlight. The horses became restless as the hours dragged on and sent shivers down Jack's spine when they shook their heads and snorted loudly in irritation at being held on a tight reign.

At last Jack caught the clink of harness and the drumming of hooves. He drew further back into the trees, not wanting to reveal his whereabouts until he had identified the riders. On reaching the crossroads the party halted and the leader, a masked man riding a rough cob, stood in his saddle and stared around him into the darkness. "You there, Mr Rattenbury?" he called quietly.

Jack left the shadows, his face masked. Holding a cocked pistol, he walked towards the group, watching for any sign of an ambush. The prisoners had been provided with clothing worn by farmers. Wide-brimmed hats, thick woollen jackets and leggings; their long riding boots were worn and scuffed. Not one item of clothing attracted attention or could be identified as *foreign*. Whoever was working for Louis had done a grand job disguising them.

"I believe one of you gentlemen is Lieutenant Michel Claude, the brother of Louis Claude?"

"Oui! Monsieur Rattenbury," said a dark, finely boned young man. He leant over the horse's mane and held out his hand in greeting. The Frenchmen stared at Jack, their bodies tensed and ready for flight. This was not the reception they had expected.

"Please dismount, gentlemen," said Jack, softening his voice in an effort to put them at their ease.

By now the two masked guides who had accompanied the prisoners were getting uneasy and desperate to leave the scene. They were only too aware that should they be discovered their involvement in the escape would cost them their lives. As soon as the Frenchmen dismounted they roughly grabbed the reins and without warning spurred the horses to a gallop and took off up through the lanes towards Tiverton.

Jack led the four men into the copse towards the waiting horses. He could see from their white, drawn faces that they were traumatised by their experience and bade them mount quickly.

"We must waste no time, gentlemen. I have found a place of safety for you and the sooner you are there the better it will be for all of us. Until we arrive I would ask that you remain silent."

Jack's knowledge of the French language was untutored but, in the way of the French upper classes, Michel could speak English fluently. He nodded his head, having understood Jack's instructions and the group set off through the lanes towards Beer.

It took an hour to reach the quarry entrance. Jack had taken a direct route, knowing every single dip and bend in the path; even so, he stopped frequently, listening for sounds of pursuit. At last they reached the track which turned into the back of the quarry. Indicating silence, Jack signalled for the riders to dismount and after tethering the horses, led the men through the low entrance.

"Wait," said Jack quietly. "This is rocky and steep. I'll light a candle."

The light flickered from the tiny flame and the Frenchmen could see that they were being taken underground. "This is part of a quarry, Lieutenant Claude, a place where rock is hewn. Please ask your men to be silent, as echoes travel through these underground workings and could lead to your discovery."

"But what of the arrangements for our return to France, Mr Rattenbury?" said the lieutenant, his voice shaking.

"Sir, what you have embarked on is a very risky undertakin'. There will be militia watching this coast for you and I don't have to tell you what will happen if we get caught. I have to wait until it's safe to move you down into the village and onto a boat for France. Not until you have set foot on the shore of Normandy will you and your men be out of danger."

The lieutenant listened gravely, aware that, although out of captivity, their troubles were far from over.

"In the meantime, gentlemen, here are provisions to make you as comfortable as possible until the next stage of your journey can be arranged."

The men stood speechless, listening hard to Jack's instructions and watched in consternation as he stumbled back up the slope, leaving them to contemplate their unenviable circumstances.

Jack heaved a sigh of relief as he left the quarry. *That's the first hurdle over*, he thought, and wearily took the horses back to the stables, all the while longing for a mug of ale and his bed.

It was now Sunday. The Rattenbury family, in line with most others in the village, observed it as a day of rest. The Lord's day, Anne called it. Anne and Hannah attended church, together with Frances and John. But Jack intended to spend some time with William talking over his plans for the coming week. The women watched and speculated as to what was going on, but neither had any idea of the dangerous situation Jack was now in.

"The best thing we can do, Hannah, is wait until it's over, whatever it is, but I have to say I've never seen Jack in such a state. He came in this marnin' just before dawn, stinking of horses, an' so exhausted he just sat in the chair and fell straight asleep."

Hannah stared into the fire, saying little. She was now swollen with a fifth child, due in four months. She looked tired and preoccupied. *He's going to get the sharp end of my tongue when I get chance to say my piece*, she thought.

Jack intended to move the Frenchmen down into the village after dark on Tuesday night. He had made an arrangement with Tom Palmer, a man known to be a friend of smugglers. For a good sum, Tom had agreed to hide the men in his attic, until Jack could get them onto his boat. The cottage stood just yards from Sea Hill. "Ask no questions, Tom, an' then you can't be accused of anythin'. These men come from Jersey, an' for whatever reason they want to get back quick. All I'm doin' is givin' them a passage home."

Tom smiled. He had known Jack since he was a child, running around selling fish with his mother. "Don't you worry, Jack, I'll look after 'em, but the sooner you get 'em on that boat the better. For some reason, the soldiers have bin everywhere these last couple of days."

For the rest of Sunday Jack wandered around the Common and down into the village with William, feeling edgy. They took John along with them after church, which was unusual, but even Jack had noticed the poisonous atmosphere in the cottage and thought it might ease the tension a bit.

"All I want you to do, William, is to make sure that boat is rigged for me to leave on Tuesday on the night tide. An' I hope the Frenchies are keeping quiet. It would be just my luck for someone to hear 'em crackin' on."

Late Monday evening Jack slipped silently into the quarry, after waiting for the lanes to empty of men returning from work. As he stumbled down into the cavern the French men jumped up in alarm.

"All right, gentlemen, it's me, Jack Rattenbury," he whispered and held up his hands to indicate that he was unarmed.

The men looked exhausted and dishevelled. "Mr Rattenbury, I am so glad and relieved to see you," said Michel. "We feared you had abandoned us."

Jack could see that the hours of sitting silently in the dark cold cavern had taken its toll on the young men. "I am sorry not to keep you informed, Lieutenant Claude, but my activities are watched closely in the village and it was too risky for me to come here in daylight."

The men were ready to forgive Jack anything as long as he could get them out of the cavern and provide a hot meal. "When can we leave, Mr Rattenbury?"

"I will take you down to a cottage in the village immediately," said Jack, "where you can rest and eat some food until it is safe to get you down to the boat."

Michel translated the plans to the other three men, who threw their arms around Jack's neck.

"Remember," said Jack gravely, "there are still many obstacles to overcome and we must stay silent and pray that we will be successful."

Jack was reluctant to take the men down through the village and so had worked out a route which avoided Fore Street. "When we leave this place, Lieutenant, I will guide you through a small wood and down through the lanes to a cottage, where you will stay for one night. The people who will care for you are trustworthy and you need have no fear of betrayal by them. When you are introduced to your hosts I will not use your military titles. From now you are Mr Claude, a potato farmer from Jersey, and these gentlemen here are your employees. Come, gentlemen, we will leave now and I beg you to keep silent."

When the group arrived at the cottage, Jack introduced them and made some play of their success in producing excellent potatoes.

"Welcome, welcome," said Tom, shaking Michel's hand. He looked curiously at the men; their clothes were soiled and their hair matted with chalk.

"I thank you for your hospitality," said Mr Claude, in correct and accent-free English.

"I've cooked you some fish," said Tom's wife, busying herself and wanting to put them at their ease. "But maybe you would care to clean your hands?" she added, making polite reference to the fact that the men's hands were filthy and caked with mud.

"Please give us food and something to drink," said Mr Claude, his voice weak with hunger. And seeing the desperate plight of the men, the table was soon covered with plates of fried fish, bread and jugs of ale.

"Looks like they've bin short of vittles for a while," remarked Tom and watched in amazement as the men threw themselves on the plates of mackerel and bread, only stopping short of eating the bones.

When they had eaten and drunk their fill, Tom brought in a bucket of water from the brook and, after cleaning themselves, the four men were taken up into the tiny attic.

"I assure you, gentlemen, it won't be a long wait," said Jack. My son is rigging the boat and, God willin', we will leave tomorrow night."

Chapter 14

Unbeknown to Jack, however, events of which he was unaware were unfolding. That day a special warrant had been issued by Exeter Magistrates Court for his arrest. The tip-off had come from Albert Rankin who, by chance, had seen Jack leading four men through the back lanes the previous night. Keeping at a good distance and hugging the shadows, he had followed the party to the cottage just off Sea Hill. Albert had wasted no time in relaying this information to the local Riding Officer who had left for Exeter at dawn to collect a warrant for Jack's arrest.

Jack spent most of Tuesday in the upstairs room of his cottage discussing avoidance tactics and escape routes with Isaac and John, two local seamen he had asked to crew for him on the trip to Cherbourg. "If we're spotted, depending on the wind, we can either cut for Weymouth or slip into Lulworth, but I'm not expecting it to be easy. It's not like running kegs. You can't just throw the buggers overboard."

"I don't know about that, Jack. If we be caught with the Frenchies, it's the hangman for us. As far as I'm concerned they can go over the side, an' to hell with 'em."

"What's that?" Jack leapt to his feet on hearing a sound at the front of the cottage.

"Are you in there, Rattenbury?" a man's voice shouted through the front window, quickly followed by a violent hammering on the front door.

"That's it! Nobody but the military punish a door like that." Jack's mind flew in all directions looking for escape, but knowing there was none.

"We're off, Jack!" Isaac and John threw themselves out of a back window, just before the front door flew open to reveal Captain Durrell flanked by several Dragoons.

Jack walked slowly down the stairs, avoiding Hannah's eyes. "I suppose it's me you're after," he said to the arresting officer.

"We are here to arrest you on the charge of attempting to smuggle prisoners of war out of the country."

Hannah gasped.

"An' what proof do you have of that?" Jack blustered, but knew full well that he had been betrayed.

The following day, Jack appeared before the Magistrates in Exeter and was not surprised to see Lieutenant Claude and his three companions in custody.

An interpreter was called to the Court and Lieutenant Claude, who was presented as the senior officer, was questioned as to how he and his companions came to be hiding in a cottage in Beer.

"Pardon?" said the Lieutenant, looking puzzled.

The Magistrate looked irritated, and hammered the bench when several onlookers in the public gallery tittered.

"Je suis desolé, monsieur, mais c'est tres difficile pour moi de vous comprendre. Je n'ai jamais rencontre Monsieur Rattenbury."

"Repeat that to me in English," said the Magistrate peering down at the flustered interpreter.

"He said, your honour, that he doesn't know why he is here and he has never met Mr Rattenbury before this morning."

At this, the gallery erupted into guffaws of laughter. The interpreter proved to be inept and his grasp of the French language was tenuous to say the least of it. After two more abortive attempts at communication, skilfully bungled by Lieutenant Claude, the Magistrate asked that the prisoners be seated.

"Silence!" he ordered, "or I'll clear the gallery. Call Mr Rattenbury," instructed the Magistrate and Jack was brought up from the cells to take his place in the dock.

"Place your hand on this Bible and swear to the Court," said the usher.

Jack looked pale and not at all the devil-may-care character who would, in times past, have cooked up an unlikely and amusing tale for the Magistrate.

"How do you explain your involvement in this affair, Mr Rattenbury?"

"Your honour, I swear on oath that I met up with these gentlemen while travelin' over to Shute to meet with Sir William Pole. I had an important letter to deliver to him and when I left his estate I was approached by these men here."

"What exactly did they ask of you, Mr Rattenbury?"

"They tol' me that they hailed from Jersey in the Channel Islands where they grow potatoes, an' that they had travelled here to Devon to visit our farmers as they wanted to buy some seed."

"I would like to put it to you, Mr Rattenbury, that you were fully aware that these gentlemen were, in fact, escaping prisoners of war and you have been caught in the act of returning them to France. A country, I am at pains to point out, with which we are still at war."

"Your honour, I would do nothin' to harm my country," said Jack, his voice rising in an effort to convince the Magistrate. "I was engaged to take the gentlemen to Jersey, of which island I thought they were natives."

Titters were again heard from the gallery and Jack looked up to see Hannah's stricken face, her eyes fixed on the back of the Court.

Captain Durrell, Lieutenant of the Sea Fencibles, stood to question Jack. He drew his shoulders back, a cynical smile playing around his lips. Over the past two years he had filed many reports to the Exeter Collector about smuggling in Beer. Jack was well known to him.

"Don't you know a native of Jersey from a Frenchman, Mr Rattenbury?"

At this point Jack's attorney leapt to his feet and deemed this an unsuitable question and advised Jack not to answer.

Captain Durrell turned to the bench in frustration, his eyebrows raised.

"Objection over-ruled," said the Magistrate. "Answer the question, Mr Rattenbury."

"I can only repeat again your honour that the gentlemen claimed they were farmers from Jersey, an' as I know they speak French in Jersey I had no reason to doubt them."

"No further questions, your honour," said Captain Durrell and returned to his seat looking like a man outwitted.

The Chief Magistrate glanced across at his colleagues and with a curt nod indicated that they wished to withdraw. "Court adjourn," said the Court Clerk. The Magistrates retired, with much scraping of chairs, to consider the verdict.

Jack had been assured by his attorney that, to his knowledge, the prosecutor had been unable to procure firm evidence of his intention to smuggle prisoners of war from the country. "Remember, Jack, they have constructed this case against you on the evidence of an informer, who claims to have seen you with four men walking up Southdown. The informer, who is known to be unreliable, admits that he was unable to see their faces and would not be able to identify them. This is not sufficient evidence on which to prosecute you. The prosecution are maintaining that you were aware that the Frenchmen were prisoners of war, but they have produced no evidence of this. Your defence that you believed you were embarking on a legal transaction, by providing transport to Jersey, is entirely feasible."

But Jack remained unconvinced and thought uncomfortably of the damning evidence contained in the quarry. Half an hour passed while Jack sat slumped in his seat, staring blankly at the floor, aware of Hannah's eyes boring into the top of his head. Rivulets of sweat ran down the back of his neck. The audience in the gallery waited with bated breath, half hoping to hear the Magistrate find Jack guilty. The case would then be transferred to the High Court, where he would undoubtedly receive the death penalty.

At last the Clerk returned, and ordered the Court to be upstanding. The Magistrates entered with due ceremony. The Chief Magistrate cleared his throat and peered at Jack over his glasses. "Following our consultation we have decided to dismiss this case owing to lack of evidence. However Mr Rattenbury, we advise you to return home and not to engage in such transactions in the future."

A stifled gasp of disappointment rose from the public gallery. Captain Durrell's face contorted into one of thunderous rage. The verdict was inexplicable, not least to Jack. He looked, with serious reflection, at the Captain's face glaring at him across the Court room. *I haven't heard the last of this,* he thought.

Hannah had only been half aware of the seriousness of Jack's situation before attending Court, having been deliberately kept in the dark, but sitting through the proceedings she had fully comprehended the possible outcome and fainted on hearing the verdict. As people ran to help her, a scuffle erupted in the gallery.

"You're nothing but a bloody traitor, Rattenbury! You should be out there doing your bit against that tyrant Bonaparte."

Jack looked up. A soldier stood facing him, waving a stick. His ragged clothes were the remains of an English army uniform.

"I lost this in the battle of Salamanca," he said, waving the stump of his right arm, "while you were swannin' around at home smuggling French prisoners out of the country. An' no doubt bein' paid a pretty penny for it."

The ushers rushed forward and forcibly ejected the man from the Court. But his voice, racked with distress and anger, echoed around the gallery as he strode off down the street.

"You're nothin' but a bloody criminal, Rattenbury! Should have been put on a man-o'-war. Justice wasn't done today in this Court."

"What has this government ever done for me or my family?" Jack muttered and pushed passed the gaolers out into the open air. But the scene had touched a nerve.

That night saw a riotous celebration in the Dolphin Inn. Isaac and John turned up looking somewhat shamefaced but thankful to see that Jack had got off.

"We had the chance of getting out, Jack, an' I know you would have done the same in our place."

Jack roared with laughter and agreed. "The times I've done that, me lads. You've got to save your own skin; we all know the risks in this game. I'll tell you what, though, if I ever find out who went running to inform on me I'll break their bloody skull!"

During the course of the night Captain Durrell strolled into the bar and looked across at Jack surrounded by his friends, most of whom were far into their cups.

"Well, look who it is," said Isaac, throwing his arm across Jack's shoulders and sneering openly in the direction of the soldier.

Jack shifted uneasily. "Keep your mouth shut, Isaac. We don't want any trouble tonight." The Captain's presence unnerved Jack and he felt the jubilation of his narrow escape slide away.

"Think I'll make for home, lads," he said, and pushed his way out of the crowded bar. By the time he had reached the Causeway Jack had sobered considerably and walked towards the cottage feeling uneasy. *I'll not let them worry me*, he thought and throwing his shoulders back swaggered into the kitchen, banging the door behind him. He sat down in front of the fire, poking the embers and threw on another log, sending an explosion of sparks up the chimney.

Hannah and Anne sat at the table in silence and completely ignored him. This wasn't what he had expected, but Hannah was determined that Jack would break first.

At last he turned and barked, "Come on, woman, say what you've got to say an' get it over with."

Suddenly, Hannah stood up, her face red with fury, and knocked her chair backwards. It hit the floor with a crash.

"I hope, Jack Rattenbury, that you are ashamed of yourself. You have put this family through hell for the past month, with your black humour an' sour looks and what for. To grub for money, smugglin' French prisoners of war. It's disgustin'. If you want my opinion the soldier in Court was right – you are a traitor, an' I'll not be able to hold my head up in this village. What's more, you've put our William in mortal danger, an' driven a wedge between us with your secrets. He hasn't sat down at this table and spoken with us for a month, nor has a smile passed his lips."

Anne sat silently, listening to Hannah give Jack what he deserved, but she doubted that many in the village would care that much. *More likely they'd be sorry for Jack that he'd got caught*, she thought.

Jack sat waiting for the tirade to end. Although he showed little of it, there was a large part of him that agreed with all that was said. He sat forward and put his head in his hands. Hannah's words stung and he felt the weight of guilt settle on his shoulders. "I only did it for you," he muttered.

But this feeble explanation brought forth a barrage of further condemnation from Hannah. "How you have got out of this with your life I'll never know. An' what was goin' to happen to us when you were swingin' from a rope?"

It was still a mystery to Jack as to how he had got off and one of the first things he would do tomorrow would be to clear that cavern of any incriminating evidence. "Where's our William?" he asked, and managed to look Hannah in the face.

"He's upstairs keepin' his head down, an' I think the least you can do is go up an' make it right with him."

Chapter 15

Hannah had had plenty of time for thinking over the past month. Under normal circumstances she enjoyed a close and loving relationship with Jack, but his silent withdrawal from her and refusal to discuss his plans had left spaces in which she travelled back and lingered on her previous life, in Lyme. Remembering that time, it was hard for her to recognise the woman she had now become.

The only child of older parents, Hannah had enjoyed a life in which she was cosseted, and care was given to her education and religious instruction. She could remember walking down Broad Street with her mother and enjoying the fawning attention shown by shopkeepers. Her father, Abraham Partridge, a pillar of society, was Master of a merchant ship called *The Wren*. Security was the word that leapt into Hannah's mind, when, lost in this reverie, she could remember no occasion when money was short in the house, or a knock on the door could mean penury.

But as she grew into a young woman Hannah's curious nature began to emerge. She felt trapped and restless in her parents' quiet house. The silence spun itself around her, stifling and oppressive. The only escape available to her was found in daydreams. Her mother called her Hannah Daydream, but she had no idea of what the dreams consisted. By eighteen Hannah was ready to break out. *Something has to happen to me in my life*, she would think feverishly, and once again lose herself by constructing unlikely adventures in her mind.

Meeting Jack was like a breath of fresh air. It happened by chance when she was walking alone by the Cobb. All around the quay were moored ships in harbour. Troop ships carrying soldiers to the wars, merchant ships of the East India Company, unloading spices from Madagascar, fishing luggers and privateers bristling with cannon. Jack was working on a boat alongside the quay and as Hannah strolled past their eyes met and, in that brief moment, Hannah was smitten. She paused, just long enough for Jack to risk calling out to her, "Lovely marnin' for a stroll, miss."

Hannah smiled and nodded but walked on to the end of the Cobb, all the while her heart racing. Each day for the next week she walked down to the quay and gradually became bold enough to reply to his cheery morning greeting. On the Friday, Jack called out, "I'm off victuallin' ships 'round the Channel Islands tonight, miss. Hope to see you when I get back next week."

Thoughts of Jack drove all else out of Hannah's mind and her mother became impatient with her daughter's lack of energy. "I do not know what will become of you, Hannah, if you can't put your mind to more practical things. You have not touched your sewing or your harpsichord for weeks." Hannah would apologise and promise to take up her former pursuits forthwith, but little changed.

On Jack's return the budding friendship continued and soon the young couple were meeting secretly. Hannah had spent her life living in a world of her own and Jack had became part of this hidden world but, after six months, she could restrain herself no longer. "I have to speak with you, Mother." Hannah's words pierced the quietness like a gun shot. Her mother looked up, alarmed at the passion and determination in her daughter's voice.

"I wish to marry a man from Beer called Jack Rattenbury." The declaration stood in the room and fell between them, opening an abyss.

Hannah's mother had been shocked to discover that her precious daughter, an apparently gentle and compliant young woman, had been leading a double life and resolutely refused to believe that she could have met up with anyone suitable while walking on the Cobb.

"We must speak to your father about this matter," she said, tears of confusion and distress coursing down her cheeks. But Hannah was determined. Attracted to Jack's flamboyant and daring personality she engaged in a long and quietly persistent campaign of gaining her father's permission to marry.

"I've made enquiries about this man Rattenbury," he said, during an evening when Hannah had pleaded piteously, "and from what I have heard he is an adventurer and not above working outside the law." But Hannah was obsessed, and by the time she had reached the age of nineteen years she had won her father over.

That all seems a very long time ago, Hannah sighed, *and I'll not deny it, these last years have not been easy; but this business with the prisoners is too much,* she thought, *and I'll not let him forget it for a long while.*

Chapter 16

Through the winter Jack kept a low profile. He had been shaken by his narrow escape and was aware that he would be under close surveillance from the military. William was soon bored and frustrated with fishing around the cove and although he kept it quiet from his mother, he often nagged Jack to get back in touch with Louis, but to no avail. "I've told you before, Will, I need to keep my head down. That bloody Durrell is out to get me one way or another. By next spring the dust will have settled a bit, an' then I'll get in touch with Louis. It's probable he's not too happy after the last muck-up anyway."

William listened impatiently but could only agree with his father. After Jack's last court appearance rumours had flown around the village like wildfire, the most unlikely one being that he was a French spy.

The village during winter was not a place to linger. Hannah often felt submerged under a welter of water when heavy mists hung over the cliffs, enclosing the valley and drifting silently through the lanes. The villagers battled to keep warm in cob and stone cottages huddled along the Causeway, roofs dripping and glowering under a heavy fringe of thatch. Some were watertight and solidly built, while others were little more than hovels. Dampness seeped through the walls and draughts crept under the ill-fitting doors.

Farms stretched over the hills towards Seaton. In springtime the fields were full of wild flowers and lambs, in winter, knee deep in mud and edged with the malodorous brook. Starre House stood in the midst of this silently alternating landscape. Solidly built of dressed Beer stone and flint, it emanated security and warmth. On her way to collect water Hannah would often gaze through the windows and speculate on the space and comfort to be found in such a house. She was now in an advanced state of pregnancy with her fifth child. There was no doubt that she enjoyed having Jack and William working around the cove and safely engaged in low-key activities within the law, but the practical difficulties of living in a tiny cottage with three adults and four children began to weigh heavily.

"Jack, this cottage is too small for all of us, an' another on the way," she complained. "Our William is now bigger'n you. An' another thing, there's a hole come in the thatch, an' the water's comin' in round the back door."

Hannah had not regained her closeness and affection for Jack following the Court appearance and despite the fact that he was not enjoying good health, suffering from a painful attack of gout, she could not sit easily with him. Jack's condition made him irritable and his general disposition was not improved by his doctor, who suggested he should cut back on the ale. But this time Jack listened patiently to Hannah's complaints and could only agree that they needed to return to their plan of building a new cottage.

"If you remember, Hannah, Mother was against any talk of knockin' this place down, but we'll put it to her that we could have it repaired an' she could stay in here, while we build the new cottage alongside. Can't see that she could object to that." Hannah smiled ruefully to herself, *Another of my ideas,* she thought. "The sooner we talk to her the better then. She's comin' in for tea soon, you speak to her."

Over the years the cottage walls, a mixture of rubble and cob, had begun to slump and wash away. Despite Jack's attempts to maintain the roof and render he'd fought a losing battle against the constant onslaught of driving rain and rising damp. Regardless of this state of affairs, Anne was happy there and determined to spend her remaining years under the same roof, leaky or not. It was Hannah who had borne the brunt of trying to care for four children in a place which felt, particularly in the middle of winter, little better than a cow barn. She felt quietly excited at the thought of a new cottage and pulled Ann onto her knee for a cuddle. "What do you think, Ann? A lovely new cottage!"

Ann looked at her mother shyly. She was now just two years old – a quiet, placid child, who was never happier than when left to sort through the button box. Hannah reflected that in comparison to some families in the village, her children were lucky. Although Jack's career was precarious, it was rare that they were ever in dire need of food, and the children were not required to work constantly in order to augment the family income. *I'll give him that*, thought Hannah. *He's taken good care of us despite the bad times.*

Frances continued to attend school for three hours every day. There was a small charge for this but Hannah was determined that she would be able to read, write and do simple arithmetic, before leaving to go into service. Hannah dreaded Frances leaving home, but enquiries had already been made for a position at Bicton House when the girl reached the age of twelve. Hannah knew that if Frances was literate she could advance herself, otherwise she'd remain a scullery maid for years.

Suddenly William burst through the door, bringing with him a flurry of cold air and a strong whiff of brine.

"We've bin' talkin' about buildin' another cottage, Will," said Hannah. "Remember, we talked about it earlier in the year, but 'things' got in the way."

Before William could answer, Anne came into the kitchen, bringing John with her and a large bag of potatoes. "These look good, Hannah, I was given 'em by John Nichols for a couple of skate. Thought they'd go down a treat with a bit of fat bacon."

Anne sat down by the fire to warm her hands and feet. "It's bitter out there; I couldn't wait to get in the dry."

"We've bin' talkin' mother," said Jack, determined not to be sidetracked. "We want to make a start on a new cottage an' I know you don't want to move out of here but we thought that if this place was repaired you could stay here and we could live in the new place alongside. What do you think?"

Anne looked surprised. She had hoped that the plans for rebuilding had been forgotten, but could see that with the new baby coming along it would soon become impossible to move around in the tiny cottage. "Sounds like a good idea to me," she said, and looking across at Hannah could see that her face was brighter than it had been in months. "Just as long as I don't have to move out of here, I'm happy," she said, and set about peeling the potatoes for tea.

Hannah was taken aback at Anne's easy compliance and made an effort to push aside the heavy weight of blackness which dogged her.

Jack stretched cautiously, his toes felt gripped in a glove of hot burning coals. "Eh, William, how about us clearing that ground tomorrow marnin'? If we put our backs into it we could get the thatch on by end October."

William was only too pleased; anything to bring some change and excitement into his life was welcome. "I'll start first thing but you'd better stay out of the way with that foot of yours. Isaac and a couple of others are at a loose end, so I'll go down later on an' see if they can come up an' give us a hand."

Jack and Hannah spent the evening talking over what size cottage they could squeeze onto the narrow plot. They agreed that the ground floor should consist of one large room, which doubled as a kitchen and living room. In the corner of the kitchen would stand a bread oven, built alongside a large inglenook fireplace, taking up most of the end wall of the building.

"This is goin' to make a big difference," said Hannah. She could see clearly in her mind's eye two spacious bedrooms under the eaves. "It won't be a grand house, but it will be better than this." Hannah quickly stopped her excited speculations, not wanting to hurt Anne.

William was out of bed early the next morning, woken by Isaac hammering on the door, irritating Jack, and raring to go. He had a good helper in Frances who was up at first light and eager to work alongside them, clearing stones and brambles. She was just eleven years old and following in her grandmother's footsteps, strong, tough and determined. She needed a tight reign not to make John's life a misery, and had already worked out his job for the day. "Get over here, John, and hold on to this shovel," she snapped as soon as he showed his face.

John was longing to be on the beach helping his grandmother sell fish, but had been given the job of picking out flint. The novelty had soon worn off but Frances kept a steely eye on him and he was expected to work hard and stick at it. His other job was to keep an eye on Ann. Luckily she was a quiet, contented girl, who liked nothing better than to sit in her large wicker basket, wrapped up in a blanket, watching the vigorous activity swirling around her. A tickle from John whenever he walked past and a dab of honey on a strip of cotton was enough to keep her smiling.

Jack's spirits picked up as the work showed signs of progress, although he was mostly supervising the activity, limping around the site, measuring out the footings and shouting orders. By the end of two days the site was clear and within five days the outline of the new cottage was in place. A neat foundation of stones, held firm with lime mortar provided the plinth for their new home.

"Good boots and a hat, that's what makes a good water tight cottage", said Jack, rubbing his hands.

A week later, Hannah wearily leant on the wooden shovel with which she was knocking up the mortar and looked over the muddy horror of a building site in winter. The rubble walls were now up three feet and ready for the windowsills and door frames to be fitted. "It's comin' on, Jack," she said, willing herself to keep going.

Jack had been unable to help with much of the labouring but had spent his time using his bartering skills. For the past week he had been surreptitiously looking over stone around the quarries and making enquiries as to how a few windowsills could find their way down the lane, without being missed. The benefactors were only too happy to oblige, on the promise of a few kegs.

"Pity we can't have a stone door frame, Hannah. Trouble is, it's too big to get down here without attracting attention, but I've got a solid oak lintel promised, an' that'll look good over the door."

There had been a mild thaw in relations over the past week or so. Hannah was distracted from her negative ruminations on Jack's character flaws and had thrown herself into mixing mortar and dreaming about how much easier life would be in a larger watertight home. "I don't care too much about the door frame but I want a good broad fireplace, an' that's goin' to need a solid length of somethin'. Also,"

Hannah added firmly, "I want some decent flagstones for the kitchen floor."

Jack leaned forward enthusiastically. "The front wall ought to be faced with knapped flint." A picture was taking place in Jack's mind of a building with more style than first planned, but Hannah rounded on him. "You just remember our circumstances, Jack Rattenbury. You haven't brought in much money for the past five months, so you can stop dreamin' about knapped flint. Any roads, we would have the whole village comin' up here to look at it, an' speculating on where you got that much money from."

Jack changed tack quickly. "You're right, Hannah," he said, looking to win a smile. "If we keep goin' like this we'll have the roof timbers up by the end of November."

And so they were. Jack opened a flagon of cider to celebrate and wasted no time in sending word to the thatcher, a Mr Jake Randall, that the trusses were in place and ready for him.

By now Hannah was weary. Her body ached and protested at the long hours of work she had put in over the past weeks. But she was determined they would move in by Christmas, in good time for the baby's arrival in early January. It took another week for the thatcher to arrive, along with two lumbering carts loaded high with neatly packed sheaves of wheat-straw. James, the Thatcher's boy helper, rode on top of the wagon.

Jack looked closely at the sheaves. Each bundle had all the ears at one end and the butt ends of the straw at the other. "Hope you've bin' careful to separate out the weeds from this lot, Mr Randall. This roof's got to last us a long while, and I want you to make sure we get a good neat combed finish."

Mr Randall ignored Jack's comments. He was used to respect from people who were only too grateful to get the job done. *Jumped-up rascal. We all know he's nothin' but a common criminal,* he thought, and gave a slight sniff of disapproval, just within Jack's earshot. "Let's get on with it, lad," he said, turning his back. "Don't want to stand round here all day when there's work to be done."

The whole of the Causeway turned out to watch the thatcher. Mr Randall worked on, oblivious to the ring of curious eyes following his every move. The Rattenburys stood among the crowd, delighted after all the hard work to see the crown of golden thatch slowly transform four stark walls and the skeleton roof timbers into a home.

It was now four weeks to Christmas and at last the fire was lit in the hearth and the family were able to spread out. The cottage smelt fragrant with the smell of straw and wood smoke. Hannah had got her flagstone floor and sat in the chair watching Frances sweep the last of the wheat dust through the door. *She's growing up fast,* thought Hannah, noting the developing curves under her daughter's blouse.

Ann was now just able to walk and tottered around the room hanging onto chairs, exploring her new home.

Hannah felt a deep weariness sink over her body. "Get me a tot of brandy, Frances. I'm not feeling too good." She let her mind wander over the past three months. *By God, it's been hard work. Don't think this one's going to last the full term.* The thought popped into her head unbidden, sending shivers of alarm down her aching legs.

That night Jack was woken by a sharp gasp. Hannah sat on the side of the bed groaning and clutching her stomach. "Tell Frances to run and get Alice, an' call your mother, I need some help," she said, and clenched her teeth together in an effort not to scream.

Frances raced down through the village, her feet barely touching the cobbles and hammered on Alice's door. Eventually a face appeared at the window. "Her's visitin' her mother in Honiton," said the face, and slammed the window. Frances ran home, pushing away the terror that her mother might die.

The hours dragged past in a nightmare of pain and fear as Hannah struggled to give birth. By morning her ordeal was over, and wrapped in a tiny shroud beside the bed was the child they had been unable to save. Hannah lay still, looking pale and exhausted, trying hard to stop the insistent black thought invading her. *This is a bad omen; our new home is cursed.*

Jack's heart went out to her as she wrestled with her grief and he made a determined effort to push the darkness from the room as it clamoured to drown them. "Hope this isn't going to bring us bad luck, Jack," Hannah sobbed, and they clung together in a desperate effort to find some human comfort in their misery.

Days passed into weeks and still Hannah did not recover her strength. She needed to repeat time and again the circumstances of her child's death, until at last Anne feared for her sanity. "You've got to find a way to get over this, Hannah. You've all your family downstairs, they need you. An' little Ann's grieving terrible: she can't understand what's happened."

Hannah listened to her mother-in-law's words; they sounded distant, as if heard from the bottom of a well. *I've got to get up for Christmas*, she thought and cast around in her mind to find some thread of hope.

"If you get a goose for Christmas dinner, Father, I'll have a go at gettin' it on the table. Will you help me, mother?" said Frances, in an effort to raise her mother's spirits. Hannah looked at her daughter and was thankful for her youth and enthusiasm

It was a quiet Christmas. Hannah forced herself to get up and was helped down the stairs by Frances and William. She looked around the new kitchen – it felt totally strange and alien to her. Anne had made her up a comfortable cot by the fire on which she sank thankfully. William sat down at the table with John and his father, while Frances encouraged Ann to show off her walking. At last a smile curled gently around Hannah's lips and tears slid down her cheeks at the sight of Ann's stubby legs staggering around on the flagstones.

I must make an effort for the sake of the children, she thought.

Chapter 17

The end of January came and went. Jack had recovered from the gout and was once more on the look-out for work. "It all seems bit quiet round the beach, William. Keep your ears open for anything going. I'm taking the boat over to Lyme for a few nights; see what I can pick up."

The following morning Jack stood on Lyme quay checking over his boat and looking anxiously at the sky. *Looks like a gale's coming in,* he thought. The clouds were inky, and angry gusts of wind swept in towards the harbour, driving the rigging into a snapping frenzy. Suddenly Jack heard the muffled boom of a gun from the bay. Another followed in quick succession and he jumped on to the wall to see a brig in the offing, her distress colours flying. He ran up the quay, shouting and waving his arms to attract attention.

"Come on, you lot, let's get out there."

Three seamen, well known to Jack, were sheltering under the harbour wall. They looked out into the bay with some trepidation. By now the sea had whipped into a fury, waves pounded onto the shore in a thunderous pile of white foam. "If we get her in there'll be a few shillin' in it for you," Jack told them.

Somewhat reluctantly, the men climbed into a sturdy rowing boat and set out for the brig. The full force of the wind hit the boat as they cleared the harbour and freezing spray broke over their heads as they rowed towards the stricken vessel through the mountainous waves. "Come on, get your backs into it, lads!" Jack yelled.

They came alongside the heaving vessel and Jack looked up to see the Captain hanging over the side of the gunnels, his face contorted into a mask of dread. Jack and the seamen secured the row boat and climbed up a rope ladder thrown over by a midshipman.

"Mr Rattenbury," said Jack, holding out his hand as he hauled himself onto the deck. "I'm employed as a pilot in these parts and know this coast better than most. Can I be of assistance?"

"Well, I'm a complete stranger here," the Captain gasped. "Will you please help us? She's in danger of going down." He wore the uniform of the Royal Navy but it was now soaked with sea water and his gold-braided hat was askew.

A man of tender years and experience by the look of him, thought Jack and took charge immediately. "Don't you worry, Captain. I'll do everythin' in my power to get you an' your men safely out of danger. Now, what water do you draw, sir?"

"Twelve feet, Mr Rattenbury."

"Well, I can't take you into Lyme as its low spring tides an' looks like this gale's gettin' up," said Jack. As they spoke a huge wave struck the vessel and tons of water crashed over the starboard bow. "I'll take charge now, sir," said Jack, brushing past the Captain who was hanging onto the rigging, paralysed with fear.

"Drop the top sail!" Jack shouted, fighting to be heard above the howling wind. The crew raced to carry out his orders. Men swarmed over the rigging and struggled to keep their footing on decks streaming with water. The brig slowly turned, like a wounded animal, into the wind. Timbers strained and groaned as the waves battered the prow, sending plumes of spray high into the air.

"We have to get at least five miles on out past Portland Bill, Captain, to avoid gettin' run aground. With some luck this storm will have blown itself out by marnin'."

The young man looked at Jack and could only signal his gratitude with a weak salute. The stench of vomit surfaced from below decks and the sound of retching soldiers mingled with the cries of men desperate to reach solid ground. The night wore on in a seeming endless battle with the elements. Jack watched for any change in the wind direction, and as the hours passed, he became more confident that they had taken the right course.

As Jack had predicted, the storm blew itself out during the night and by morning they found themselves in calmer waters. "Think we should drop anchor now, Captain, and rest a while. Your cargo sounds like they could do with it," said Jack, laughing at the pitiful groans of the soldiers tottering around the deck.

"Can I offer you a glass of rum?" asked the Captain, having now regained his composure and gathered around him his fellow officers to raise a toast to the men who had undoubtedly saved their lives.

Jack and his companions accepted this offer gratefully. It was when listening to the officer's report in relation to his men that Jack realised how he could turn the situation to his advantage. The brig was in fact the *Linskill*, a troop ship, carrying part of the 82nd Regiment and several of her officers back to England after fighting Napoleon's forces in Spain.

"You have done a great job, Mr Rattenbury," the Captain said, now in high good humour.

And it could not be denied that Jack had carried out an impressive rescue and saved the lives of scores of men. He turned over the sequence of events in his mind and noted the profuse and grateful thanks proffered by the Captain and the officers of the regiment. *I've got to turn this situation to my advantage,* he thought.

As the day wore on into evening, Jack made up his mind to ask the officer's advice with regard to the problems he had with Captain Durrell. "The man wants to see me behind bars or worse. Please understand, gentlemen, I have an elderly mother, four children and a wife to support. They would all starve should I not provide for them."

The men listened sympathetically to Jack's story (of which he told only half) and suggested a possible means by which he could appeal for help. "As soon as you get ashore, Mr Rattenbury, you should have printed a handbill describing what you have done on our behalf. The story can be verified and we would not hesitate to confirm it. Please accept this guinea for the cost of printing."

Jack was pleased with this solution. Surely the declaration that he had taken a major part in saving eighty men of the 82nd Regiment could not be ignored. "When they know about this perhaps they'll get off my back and allow me to get back to earning an honest living," he declared.

At noon the brig set sail in the direction of the Isle of Wight. Jack skilfully guided the *Linskill* into the Needles, where the Captain took on another pilot. "Before you leave, Mr Rattenbury, here is twenty guineas for your services and many thanks for your help and assistance," he said. "There is no doubt in my mind that but for your excellent seamanship we would now be at the bottom of Lyme Bay."

Jack paid his companions a generous cut and they all set out for Lyme on a cargo boat delivering coal. The money felt good in his pocket and he harboured the hope that a way had been found to outwit Durrell.

Arriving home that night Jack had an exciting tale to tell. "Look what I've got here," he said proudly. He looked up to see Hannah smiling, and for the first time in many a long month there was colour in her cheeks. "This is what the Captain gave me." Jack pulled the paper out of his pocket. "Read it out to us, Hannah."

This is to certify that Jack Rattenbury, pilot of Beer, near Axminster, was of great service to the brig Linskel Transport, in assisting her out of a perilous situation on the 24th instant by getting on board her off Lyme; and saved her from foundering off Abbotsbury Beach, having on board part of the 82nd Regiment of Foot, from Spain.

Witness Major McDonell and Capt G Marshall.

"I'm goin' to get this notice put in the *Exeter Flying Post* and do what Captain Marshall says an' print out some handbills."

Chapter 18

What Jack had failed to disclose to Captain Marshall was that he was still on the run from H.M. Navy. The offence of desertion had taken place some years back, before John was born. Jack had managed to avoid arrest by being continually on the move, and finally by removing himself from seafaring altogether and opening the public house. This somewhat desperate solution had provided him with cover for a few years, but with Durrell and the Dragoons now stationed in the village it was getting difficult to avoid the matter being discovered.

"We've got to think hard on this one, Hannah. There's no doubt about it, that last court appearance has stirred up Durrell's interest in me an' it's only a matter of time before he discovers I'm a wanted man."

William and Anne leant forward over the table. "I know we've heard it all before, Jack, but tell it to us again," said Anne laughing. The family gathered around and waited in eager anticipation. They all knew the story by heart but it never failed to grip them.

Jack poured himself a mug of cider and let his mind wander back. "One night, I was on the way back from Alderney with a few kegs, when I was pulled up by the Excise. The Captain was a real gentleman he was, a real gent. He called for me to be brought to his cabin and invited me to sit down with him for a good roast meal. Beef, if I remember rightly. He introduced me to his officers and, thank God, I hadn't come across any of 'em before. 'Eat up, Mr Rattenbury,' he said, an' kept my glass filled. We had a right merry evening. He wanted to know about my life as a smuggler. I told him a bloody good story, mark my words, but took good care not to give away too many secrets. We was all bladdered by the time I was sent back down below.

"The following morning we'd reached Cowes harbour an' I was brought up on deck, expecting to be given a warning and set ashore, but that was not to be." Jack paused for dramatic effect. "The Captain, he turned to me an' said, 'Rattenbury, I'm going to send you aboard a man-o'-war.'

"He was so polite an' spoke in a quiet gentlemanly voice, I couldn't believe my ears. Just then a cutter came alongside carrying a lieutenant of H.M. Navy and several ratings. You could have knocked me down with a feather. 'Sir,' I said, addressing the Captain, 'you have given me roast meat ever since I came aboard and now you have run the spit in me.' The oily rascal just smiled.

"Mr Rattenbury,' he said, 'we are at war and the Navy need men like you. Do your duty for the sake of your country.'

'A pox on that,' I shouted and made to jump over the gunnels but it was no good. Three men brought me down and had me clamped in irons before I had a chance. I felt pretty sick, I can tell you."

The family were now clustered around Jack and drinking in his every word.

"What 'appened then?" said Frances breathlessly.

"Well, after moving me about a bit they put me aboard the *Resistance,* a man-o'-war bound for Portsmouth, an' from then on to Ireland. The boat was packed with smugglers and many other poor buggers they'd managed to grab. Some of 'em had been on there for a year or more. I knew most of 'em but, by luck, none of the officers recognised me."

Hannah and William knew the story from start to finish but encouraged Jack to go on.

"What was it like on the man-o'-war"?

"No other words for it, bloody terrible. When they opened the hatches the stench hit your nose like a midden. Men were packed cheek by jowl, 'bout eighty in all. At the end of the deck stood an iron range, where the food was cooked. Mostly it was horrible rancid gruel and such like but on the trip over to Ireland they took on a few sheep, for fresh meat. The smell and racket from them was terrible. It took us eight days to get to Cork and thank God the weather was fair, the Irish Sea can be the very devil. Even so, by then I'd had enough of it. You had to fight for your food, fight for your grog, fight to get some sleep, it was like being locked in a hell hole. But you know me well enough, I can't stand being trapped and set out to find a way to get out of it."

"You're right there, son," said Anne and laughed, looking at Hannah knowingly.

"My first go at getting off didn't work; they had guards stationed every twenty yards round the boat. It looked darn near impossible. But the next day, I noticed the ship's lighter coming alongside to deliver water. There was men running backwards and forwards all over the place, hauling up the casks and when the guard's back was turned I jumped in the lighter holding an empty cask, an' that way passed myself off as a crew man."

Will laughed and clapped his father on the back. "You're a slippery one, an' that's for sure, Father."

"That's how I managed to get away, an' when I got ashore I ran like hell." Jack took a long draw on his cider. "I tell you, I'll never hear a word against the Irish, they saved my life that day."

"Well, I've heard you cuss 'em a few times."

"That may be so, Will, but on that day there's no doubt about it, they saved my life. This woman spotted me hiding in a hedge. It was obvious that I wasn't a local but she took me in and gave me a good feed. Her husband was very sympathetic to my plight, an' sent their son into Cork to see if he could pick up some news. When he came back that night he said the place was alive with marines, looking for the captain of the smugglers, who had escaped."

"That's a laugh," said Hannah. "Captain of the smugglers!"

"Well, anyway," said Jack, ignoring the slight tone of ridicule in Hannah's voice, "I hired a gig from the family and got to Youghal, where in the harbour I passed myself off as the captain of a vessel, and had the good fortune to find a boat bound for Weymouth. All in all it took me six days to get home and it was a joy to see your mother an' you all again."

"That's a good story," said Hannah, "but I can tell you it wasn't a good time for me with you away, an' me not knowin' when you would turn up, but you've not said about the best bit."

Jack laughed. "That was amazin'. Sometimes I think I must have nine lives.

"Somehow word had got 'round that I was back in the village and they sent some constables to the cottage to arrest me as a deserter. I got away that time and laid low. The village was alive with his men looking for me, so I made off and spent the next month doin' runs to Alderney out of Lyme, and bloody successful they were an' all," Jack said pointedly, looking at Hannah. "One night, after about a month, I went back into Beer to catch up with some of me old mates. I was in The Dolphin with Abe, Jim, Isaac and a few others when this bloke, Sergeant Hill was his name, came in with about a dozen Dragoons. They was armed to the teeth with swords and muskets. My guts ran to water, I can tell you. I knew that if they got me I'd have to 'go through the fleet'."

"What's that?" a voice piped up. Hannah looked round and John was sitting at the bottom of the stairs, hoping not to be noticed.

"It's somethin' I hope you'll never suffer," said Jack, and allowed him nearer the fire. "Three hundred lashes of a cat-o'-nine-tails, that's what it is. They takes you round every ship in the fleet and you get twenty-five lashes from each one. I've known men have it but not many recover to tell the tale. Anyway, this Sergeant came towards me an' shouted out that I was a deserter and he was arresting me. I tried to talk my way out of it, tellin' him he'd made a mistake but he wasn't havin' it. I was bloody desperate by then I can tell you, so I ripped off my shirt, so as they had nothin' to hold me with, grabbed a reap hook, stuck a knife in my pocket an' jumped down the steps leading into the cellar."

A spontaneous cheer erupted from the family. "What 'appened then?"

"Well, if it wasn't so serious it would have been comical, 'cause, having heard the ruckus, the bar started to fill up with locals and the soldiers looked round to see that they was surrounded. There's none that can look as evil as a bunch of

Beer men when one of their own is in a tight corner. Every way out was blocked.

"To give him his dues the Sergeant stood his ground. He was determined to get me this time. I waved the reap hook around an' shouted at the top of my lungs. 'See this? I'll kill the first bugger who comes near me.' He was tryin' hard not to lose his nerve.

"Come on, do your duty and take him!' he shouted at his men. His face was getting redder an' redder. The soldiers shuffled forward but so did the crowd, pressing right in behind 'em. 'If you come near me I'll rip your guts out,' I said, looking him right in the eye. The crowd, led by Abe Mutter, roared and stamped their feet. They was ready for a fight. It was a stand-off. The soldiers knew that if they did take me they'd have a job getting out of the village in one piece. Suddenly a screechin' started up at the back of the pub and a gang of women ran in, kicking up one hell of a racket. What I found out later was that your mother, havin' been told of my plight by Abe, had cooked up a story with Jane Bartlett and a few others."

"I kept out of it," said Hannah, taking up the story, "but Jane's got a voice like a foghorn an' went in there shouting her head off. 'Help, help! There's a boy in the sea, just off shore, an' he's drownin'. Come on, you lot."

"The soldiers didn't need any encouragement, as by then the whole village was breathin' down their necks," Jack continued. "They ran off down the beach, Sergeant Hill close behind, an' that gave me the opportunity to get out the back way an' down to Seaton Hole, where your mother had a row boat ready. When I got out to the lugger I couldn't resist hoisting the colours before leaving the bay. Stupid beggars, taken in by a bunch of women! "So you see, Will, when I came up in court over the Frenchies, it was unbelievable that I got off. Somebody is looking after me. Now I've got this handbill I'm goin' to see if I can get a pardon from Lord Rolle; I've done him enough favours over the years."

Jack took a deep breath and sighed. "All that happened about five years ago; since then I've kept out of the way of the Navy. Most of 'em will turn a blind eye for a keg or a backhander, but you've always got to be on the look-out for the others."

Hannah was quiet and thoughtful. She looked around the hearth at Jack's mother and the children, their faces lit by the firelight all wrapt in the excitement of their father's adventures. *There's not a dull bone in his body,* she thought, shaking her head.

Chapter 19

"I'll just go down to see Molly at the school, an' find out when Lord and Lady Rolle will be visitin'," said Hannah.

Jack looked intently at the handbill, although unable to read it. "This should help my cause and show him that I'm loyal to my country. I just hate being in the Navy, and anyway, I'm more usefully employed round here looking after my family," he complained bitterly to Hannah. "Trouble is, this bloody war is going on and on, an' that's all the government can think of. We need to finish Napoleon once and for all, but he's a tough bugger to crack."

Hannah, for once, was sympathetic to her husband's plight. "There's no doubt Lord Rolle has the power to help you, if he's a mind. Somebody told me he's Commander of the Devon militia. If I can get him to read that handbill it would all be sorted out when he sees what you've done."

Spring had quietly crept into the village, lifting the mists and edging the brook with yellow celandines and daisies. Hannah had regained her strength following the loss of the baby and was now happy to work around the cottage, tending the garden and encouraging Frances to pursue her interest in lace-making.

The girl smoothed out a simple lace collar, now in the finishing stages. "I should get a couple of pennies for this, Mother," she said proudly and bent industriously over her lace pillow. The bobbins clattered. "One to the right, two to the left and one over." Frances repeated the instruction rhythmically.

Hannah smiled. She was proud of her daughter, who was her constant companion and had been her rock during the long winter months.

"I've heard that Lord and Lady Rolle are coming to the village tomorrow and I intend standing outside the school to see if they will take notice of this handbill. It might help if you stood alongside me."

Frances cringed. The thought of her mother bringing attention to their plight in front of the whole school made her blush with alarm. "Do I have to be there, Mother?" But Hannah was not to be deterred and was well aware that with a child beside her she could bring more sympathy to bear on Jack's cause.

Mother and daughter were standing outside the school gates early, and soon after ten the clattering wheels of a carriage could be heard coming down the Causeway. Frances attempted to shrink into the background, but as the carriage came to a halt Hannah stepped forward, firmly holding her daughter's hand. The door opened, held by a footman, and Lady Rolle stepped down onto the forecourt of the school, followed by his Lordship.

I've got to do it now, thought Hannah and pushed herself forward. "Lord Rolle, I would ask you to read this handbill. It concerns my husband. We are greatly in need of your assistance." Hannah's voice held steady and clear.

His Lordship took the handbill and promised to read it while he was waiting for his wife, who by this time had walked on into the school.

Children stood in neat lines and looked in awe at the finely dressed couple. The teachers stood woodenly, unable to relax in the presence of their benefactors or to respond to her ladyship's efforts to put them at their ease. Lady Rolle made a habit of wearing Beer lace and that morning wore a particularly fine bonnet with a fall made by women in the village. She smiled and nodded and looked with interest at the slates on which the children had produced their best handwriting for her inspection.

"This is very neat," she said to Benjamin, son of the vicar, who had been chosen for his quiet demeanour and tidy appearance. The boy stood as if turned to stone.

"Say thank you to your ladyship," the teacher hissed.

Lord Rolle stood on the sidelines, reading the handbill and looking thoughtful.

A flurry of handshakes and grateful thanks told Hannah that the visit was coming to an end. "Here they come, Frances. Smile nicely."

Lord Rolle stepped out into the lane, carefully avoiding the brook, which was in full flood from the spring showers. "Where is the woman who was speaking to me about her husband?"

Hannah stepped forward. "It was me, your Lordship." She glanced up to see Lord Rolle looking down at her with a pensive look.

"I am sorry, Mrs Rattenbury, I can't do anything for your husband because, if I remember rightly, he is the man who threatened to cut my sergeant's guts out while resisting arrest."

Hannah looked crestfallen. He pressed the handbill back into her limp hands and strode down into the village to inspect the Dragoons waiting on Sea Hill. Hannah and Frances ran home to tell Jack what had happened.

"I think you ought to have a go. Her Ladyship's carriage is going past the cottage in a minute."

Jack ran outside, determined not to miss this chance of putting his case. He had spent the winter laying low and consequently the family were now in dire need of funds. He stood in the lane, tense and waiting for the first sound. At last he could detect the creak of the carriage moving slowly up the Causeway. As it reached the cottage Jack threw himself in front of the horse, which reared back whinnying in alarm. The coachman swiftly drew the carriage to a halt.

"What the bloody hell do you think you're doing?" the driver shouted.

Her Ladyship looked out of the window to see Jack, covered in mud, holding out his handbill.

"I'm sorry to inconvenience you, your Ladyship, but I entreat you to use your influence with his Lordship on my behalf. I am loyal to my country and as you will see from this handbill I saved the lives of many men of the 82nd Regiment who were aboard the *Linskill* when they were returning to this country after fightin' in Spain."

Lady Rolle looked alarmed, but Jack held her attention and impressed her with his polite and sincere manner. "I love goin' to sea, your Ladyship, but I have an aversion to the Navy and wish to remain with my wife and family. We have recently lost a child and she needs my support." Jack waited, watching her eyes and trying to gauge her reaction.

"Mr Rattenbury, you have such a fighting spirit, it would be well used in the service of your country. Go back on a man-o'-war and be equal to Lord Nelson. If you do so, I will take care that you shall not be hurt."

At this Jack fell to his knees and repeated doggedly, "I must support my family in a creditable manner, I cannot think of returning to the Navy." Jack had now said his piece and could think of no other way to impart his desperation. He waited, their eyes locked.

"I will consider it." This was said in a near whisper and Jack was surprised to see her eyes fill with tears.

Within a week the soldiers were ordered to leave Beer.

"I'll be bloody glad to get out of this godforsaken village," one was heard to complain. "It's impossible to catch this lot out. False trails, false information, they've got it all worked out – a right wiley lot, they tie us up in knots." His sidekick grunted. "Even use their ratbag children to get messages through the village an' light warning fires. What can you do against that? A pox on 'em, that's what I say."

Jack wasted no time in getting back to sea. He had an enthusiastic partner in Will who couldn't wait for some excitement. "It's still goin' to be difficult, Will, they keep telling us the war will be over this year but there's no sign of it yet."

Will had no patience with talk about the war. He was now fourteen years old and the war with the French had been going on for as long as he could remember. "We can't let that stop us. There's still lots of ways to get the stuff across and in the meantime we can pick up on some good cargo runs."

"Probably a good idea to work away from Beer for a bit, Will," said Jack cautiously. "I'll start looking around Weymouth, we're not so well known around there."

Chapter 20

Five years had now passed since Jack had been provided with the chance of a fresh start by Lord Rolle. An opportunity was given, by this magnanimous gesture, for a new life, an escape from smuggling into a law-abiding and less risky existence but, true to form, Jack was drawn relentlessly back into smuggling runs and constant confrontations with the excise patrols.

The twenty-year war with Napoleon was over. The long struggle to defeat Bonaparte had left the country exhausted, distressed and impoverished. Bread riots were not unknown in the streets of Exeter. The excise cutters were patrolling the coasts in greater numbers, bent on increasing the depleted coffers of a country on its knees. The dangers of dealing in contraband had never been more evident. But for Jack, William and, increasingly, John smuggling continued to be part of their lives and with the country in such a parlous state, the struggle to support a family was ever more difficult.

Hannah continued to be surrounded by children and constantly grieved for Frances who had left the family home three years back to work in service at Bicton House. Anne remained a constant. She worked hard around the beach selling fish, and helped Hannah care for the younger children, of whom Abraham was now her favourite.

By the end of December 1820 Jack and his sons had suffered a series of disasters, the worst being the loss of their largest boat, the *Elizabeth and Kitty,* which was wrecked off Abbotsbury beach during a storm. But another danger threatened. Enemies are made in a life packed with violent subterfuge and Jack had made one such enemy with the name of Cowley. This man had, in the hope of avoiding impressment, offered the collector at Exeter information concerning a cargo of spirits Jack had required him to bring in from Cherbourg. By a succession of cunning manoeuvres,

Jack had escaped capture on this occasion, but was finding it increasingly difficult to maintain his ebullient nature in the face of constant and unremitting pursuit by the excise men.

"I'm gettin' worn down, Will," he complained to his son one morning. "A gentleman on the beach asked me if I was interested in takin' him out fishin' during the summer, an' I think that's what I'm goin' to do. Our John wants to join us, an' it would do him good to get away from mother."

William was happy with this suggestion. For several years now he had been itching to take over his father's boat and had gathered around him a gang of men who were always up for doing a run, no matter how risky. But they were also under constant surveillance and it would be only a matter of time before William would see the inside of Dorchester gaol.

But Jack's decision to keep a low profile for the summer had come too late. One evening he was up on the cliffs with John and his youngest son, Abraham, keeping a look-out for a string of kegs dumped in the cove, when he was approached by the mate of the *Scourge*, an excise cutter anchored in the bay.

"Mr Rattenbury, good evening to you," said the mate. "I have a spyglass belonging to you aboard, it's been there for a few months, but we've not crossed each other's path of late."

Jack looked at the man warily, but he continued with his easy pleasantries and was curious to know more about life in Beer.

"I've heard the fishermen round here cannot be beaten, Mr Rattenbury. Tell me, what secrets do they have for spotting the herring shoals, which I've heard come here in great numbers?"

Jack did not intend giving away anybody's secrets, not least the fishermen's, but slowly warmed to the man and they sat in companionable conversation while the boys played and tumbled in the grass. Eventually it was time for the mate to leave and Jack bade him farewell.

"I'll come out later, sir, and collect my spyglass," said Jack

That evening Jack took his row boat and, together with his two young sons, paid a visit to the *Scourge*. He was welcomed aboard and made most comfortable. "Please come into my cabin," said the Captain, after keeping Jack waiting for some time, "and I'll return your property."

No sooner was Jack through the door than he realised he had been set up. Standing beside the captain was a deputation officer holding a warrant for his arrest.

"We are arresting you on information given to us by John Cowley, captain of the Lyme packet, a vessel you chartered to transport contraband from Cherbourg in November of last year."

Jack stood dumbfounded and started to shake with rage.

"What would you like done with your boys, Mr Rattenbury?" continued the Captain smoothly.

"Throw 'em overboard if you like an' drown 'em. You've taken their father from 'em with your dastardly trick."

But shout and struggle as he may, Jack was neatly caught. Arrangements were made for his sons to be returned to the shore and he was taken to Exmouth and then on by carriage to Exeter gaol.

After spending some months in Exeter, Jack was taken to London under armed guard to stand trial, but despite the best endeavours of his counsel he was sentenced to one year's imprisonment.

It was a long and gloomy journey back to the West Country, giving Jack much time to contemplate his fate. "It's not goin' to be easy to talk my way out of here," he thought, as the vast iron-studded gates of Exeter gaol closed behind him with a dull thud, designed to make the stoutest heart sink.

Jack was not a stranger to Exeter gaol but on previous occasions he'd been confident of an early release and this had been granted after energetic applications by his able barrister, Mr Tyrell. But times had changed. The Government was determined to make an example of intransigent smugglers and Jack could certainly be counted as such.

"Get your arse in there, Rattenbury," said the warder, giving Jack a kick and vigorously slamming the cell door. He stood back looking at Jack through the bars, a sardonic sneer stretching across his lips.

Jack turned abruptly with his fists up, but quickly let them drop, recognising the desperate situation he was in and knowing better than to mark himself out as a troublemaker.

Months passed, punishing Jack with the tortuous knowledge that each day would be the same and that each day would consist of inedible food, constant mind-destroying work and incarceration in a crowded, malodorous cell, without light or warmth. Freedom – how he longed for it, and vowed, once again, that he would live within the letter of the law when gaining his liberty.

Visitors were rare and Jack received only two such during his year of imprisonment. Anne came on one occasion and Hannah on another. The journey to Exeter was arduous and Hannah was four months into her seventh pregnancy when Jack was arrested. Despite her condition Hannah left no stone unturned in her efforts to achieve an early release for her husband.

"I've sent letters to everyone I can think of, Jack," she said during her only visit, in an attempt to raise his spirits, "but so far I haven't had a single reply. Thank God our William is able to help us; otherwise I don't know where we'd land up."

Jack could only sit with his head bowed, bereft of the energy to make one of his impassioned declarations of his intention to lead a blameless life, if only he could be granted his release.

Precisely to the day, one year after he was sentenced, Jack was led to the main gate and stood impatiently as the warder completed his release document.

Bastard, Jack silently cursed the official who was taking his time and needlessly dragging out the procedure. After what seemed a never-ending wait, the impenetrable door opened and Jack walked outside into Queen Street. He stood in stunned confusion, overwhelmed by the noise and continual stream of carriages clattering over the cobbles.

"Thought you'd like a ride, me old mate," shouted Abe over the din.

Jack looked around, recognising a familiar voice. Cautiously he picked his way across the street strewn with garbage and horse droppings.

"This is good on yer, Abe, I didn't expect anybody," he said, climbing up beside his friend. "Thank God I'm out of that 'orrible place. You wouldn't put a dog in there, it's a bloody disgrace."

Abe nodded his head, noting Jack's pallor and handed him a flagon of cider.

"Can't understand why they don't just leave us alone. We don't harm nobody – well, not unless they gets in our way, that is."

Abe laughed. "I wouldn't say that, Jack. If you'd seen yourself in The Dolphin that night, when the Dragoons was after you, enough to frighten the life out of a man."

"That's different, they'd got me cornered," said Jack, rubbing his nose and smiling at the memory.

Abe wasted no time in getting out of the city and onto the coastal road. The April weather was flickering into warmth; the fields were bravely greening up and an opalescent sun hung over the sea, sending a soft apricot glow rippling into the shore. "Look at that – beautiful," said Jack, breathing in the soft fresh air. "Can't tell you how much I missed putting out to sea. All you got to look at in there is four walls, an' the faces of all the other miserable wretches. I spent every day for the past twelve months pickin' oakum, or walking a treadmill. 'Nuf to drive a man into madness. Anyway, I want to put that behind me. What's the news in the village?"

Abe stopped at Hangman's Stone, relieved to get away from the stench of prison, which hung around Jack like an open drain.

"I shall be wantin' to get back to work, Abe," said Jack, jumping down from the cart with surprising sprightliness. "Keep me in mind for anythin' that's goin'. Our Will's managed to keep a boat runnin', Hannah tells me, so we've got somethin' to work with."

Ann had been waiting at the top of the lane for sight of her father since early morning. "He's comin'!" she shouted, on spotting Jack striding along the path. She ran into his arms and he swung her around, marvelling at how tall she had grown in the past year.

The cottage was bursting with family and friends by the time they reached home. "Hannah," Jack whispered. He felt his chest tighten. "You look a picture, an' a different shape to when we last met."

Hannah laughed, and savoured the relief of seeing Jack home and filling the cottage again with his booming laugh. "Look here, Jack, we've another girl. I'd like to call her Mary Anne, if that's all right with you?"

Jack nodded, "You can call 'er anythin' you like, Hannah."

Anne sat watching her son. She too was overjoyed to see him home, but as was her way she kept her distance and smiled quietly while pouring him a cup of ale.

Jack sat down at the table and looked around the kitchen. *No one will know*, he thought, *how beautiful this all looks after the months spent in that rotten, stinking dump.* "Looks like you've done a good job looking after the family while I've been away, Will," he said.

John scowled and noted that, as usual, William got any praise going.

"I've done my fair share, Father. We've all mucked in, even John."

John was now ten years of age. The demanding and destructive side of his nature had mellowed a little. That is not to say he was entirely happy with his lot. William dominated the family when Jack was away.

Things'll change now that father's home, thought John. *It's always better when he's here.*

They sat down to a meal of fried skate wings and potatoes and Hannah set about bringing Jack up to date on all the family gossip and events he had missed during the past year.

"I've got some cargo runs lined up," said Will, "an' John's bringin' in some good hauls of fish, so we haven't starved. That bein' said, we need to build up some funds if we want to get in on the big money. Plenty of runs goin' over to France, but it's hot, the excise men is everywhere."

Jack spent the next six months fishing around the cove with John and picking up information on any work that might be in the offing. Never had life tasted so sweet.

Chapter 21

"Somebody at the door for you, Jack," shouted Hannah.

Standing outside was a young boy who had been sent with a message. "Dr Palmer wants you to come up to his house in Colyton, Mr Rattenbury. He said, if you could come tomorrow morning at ten o'clock he would be waiting for you."

Jack was intrigued. *The only reason he'd want to see me,* he thought, *is if they needs some grog.*

The boy waited patiently.

"Well, you can tell Dr Palmer, I'll be there prompt and give him my good wishes."

Jack walked up through the lanes to Colyton the following morning pondering on what a man like Dr Palmer would want with him.

The doctor lived in an imposing Georgian house, just off the square, with a brightly polished brass door knocker. Jack gave the door a firm rap, which brought a swift response from the maid.

"How's it goin' here, Kitty?" said Jack, recognising a young girl from the village.

Kitty flushed, the colour creeping above her white collar. "It's all right, Mr Rattenbury, but I miss me mam. I don't get down to Beer very often."

Hearing voices, Dr Palmer opened the door to his study.

"Good morning to you, Mr Rattenbury. Please come in. May I introduce you to Major Still and Major Pine. I expect you are wondering what this is all about. Please take a seat, won't you, and we'll have some tea. I'm sure you are hot and thirsty after your walk."

Jack accepted readily but watched and waited, not wanting to make any false assumptions.

Leaning comfortably back in his chair Dr Palmer stretched his hands over his copious stomach and smiled.

"I don't know if you are aware of it, Mr Rattenbury, but the construction of a ship canal is planned, between Beer and Bridgwater Bay, and in addition an extensive harbour is to be constructed in Beer cove. We need your advice on sea conditions off the East Devon coast."

Jack's jaw dropped. *Bloody hell!* he thought. *Hope there's somethin' in this for me,* and sat forward eagerly in his chair.

Dr Palmer smiled broadly, noting Jack's interest. "As you can see, this will be a very big undertaking and we need specialist information, which is to be submitted to a Committee of Enquiry at Westminster. The man gathering such information is Sir William Pole."

Jack's mind skittered in all directions. The need to make money was paramount and he was determined to make the most of this opportunity, but the link with Louis and the possible connection with the escape of the French prisoners also exercised his brain.

He straightened his back and watched the three men with rapt interest, caught between need and his instinct to get out.

Dr Palmer was totally unaware of the turmoil spinning around in Jack's head and benignly carried on explaining the purpose of his involvement. "Sir William is convinced that you are the man with sufficient knowledge of the coast to help us make a good case for the Committee," he continued. If you are in agreement, Sir William has asked us to visit him at Shute House this morning, in order that he can question you further." Jack nodded his agreement, and swallowed the last dregs of tea sweetened with sugar – a rare treat.

The gig was brought to the front of the house. As Jack climbed in the back he marvelled, *One minute I'm in a poxy gaol, running with stinking water an' rats an' the next – well, its bloody amazin'.* The horse's hooves clicked sharply through the stony lanes on the way up to Shute. On this visit Jack had no trouble getting past the guard on the gate, who stood back and saluted Dr Palmer as they swished past and up to the front door.

"Ah, here is Rob Roy come again," Sir William shouted from the top of a wide marble staircase, and made his way down, wheezing and coughing, into the hall.

"Come in. Come in, gentlemen, and we'll get some refreshment."

Sir William led the four men into a large and comfortable study. Jack looked around curiously at the walls lined with books. In the middle of the room stood a polished walnut table on which lay a detailed map of the East Devon coast.

"I doubt that few know this coast better than you, Mr Rattenbury," said Sir William, a knowing smile hovering around his lips. "We are looking at several possibilities for improvements along the coast – the first being a harbour in Beer, and also, as I believe Dr Palmer and the gentleman here has mentioned, a ship canal from Beer to either Stolford or Bridgwater Bay. This canal is intended to link up the Bristol and English Channels and I'm sure you can see the advantage of that. What we are interested in is the depth of the sea at various points, and the difficulties experienced by vessels around Portland, but, first things first."

He rang the bell for the maid.

"Nellie, bring in a decanter of my finest brandy for Mr Rattenbury. I'm sure he would appreciate a wee dram, as the Scots say."

The five men stood poring over the maps, quietly savouring the smooth amber liquor. Jack cupped the delicate cut-glass brandy bowl in his palm.

"First time I've tasted brandy from a glass, Sir William. Usually comes straight out of the keg."

They all laughed heartily. "And may you keep it coming, Mr Rattenbury, it's greatly appreciated. And now to business. I expect Dr Palmer has explained that you would need to spend some time in London. I trust this would be agreeable to you? Lord Rolle, with whom I am sure you are familiar, will be attending the meeting in Westminster and will take care of your expenses."

Jack nodded enthusiastically, still reeling at the turn of events. "I be ready to go today, sir, but I would need to send a message to my family."

"Certainly," said Sir William and summoned the boy to inform Mrs Rattenbury that her husband would be away in London for a few days. "You can tell her that there's nothin' to worry on," said Jack, aware that Hannah would be likely to jump to conclusions over his sudden disappearance.

"I'll arrange for you to be taken to Chard," said Sir William. "The mail coach leaves tomorrow morning and tonight you can sleep in the George and Dragon. I'm sure you'll be well looked after by Mrs Flannery. And here, take this, a guinea for your time."

The mail coach left Chard at 4a.m. The fields were covered in heavy dew but the soft sweet smell of an early May morning filled the coach and diluted the unwelcome odours emanating from Jack's fellow travellers. Few people or carts were in the lanes at that hour and with enthusiastic use of the whip and shouts of encouragement the coachman kept the horses at a steady trot. The coach bumped and jarred over the ruts, setting up a racket from its tortured springs so deafening that conversation was impossible. Jack's fare was paid by Sir William, which gave him a seat inside the coach, but by the time it reached Reading, late in the evening, he wondered if this was not a mixed blessing. Six passengers were squeezed cheek by jowl into the swaying carriage and the two ladies present held handkerchiefs over their noses in an effort to avoid the noxious fumes spewed out from the clay pipes enjoyed by the male passengers.

A blast of the horn signalled their arrival at the Crown Inn, where Jack had a bed for the night. He was relieved to get out and stretch his legs. The arrival of the mail coach in Reading always attracted interest and many of the townspeople gathered around, wanting to pick up news. Jack stood and watched as the stable boys unhitched the horses.

"Ladies and gentlemen, your dinner is waiting," called the landlord, ushering the weary passengers into the dining room. Hot bowls of mutton stew, with jars of frothing ale, were brought to the table. Jack ate with good appetite. He had yet to regain his physical health after the year spent in Exeter gaol. Later on in the tap room he watched the armed mail guard with interest and made it his business to strike up a conversation.

"Get many highwaymen on this route?"

The guard looked Jack over with a slight air of suspicion and didn't answer directly. "And where are you from, sir?"

Jack told him he was a seaman from a small village on the coast and was going to London on business for Sir William Pole.

"Well, sir, at the moment it's easier since the new toll road opened. Even so, about one chancer a week has a go. The horses can really get going now the road's better. Not so easy to stop us then, you see."

Jack relaxed back into his chair feeling pleasantly full and pleased with himself. "The bastards ought to be strung up if you ask me. I've no sympathy with men who would terrify women and chillern. They're nothin' but common criminals," he said.

The coach left the next morning at 4a.m. prompt. Jack stared out over the changing countryside as the coach sped along the main road towards London. By daylight it was teeming with travellers of all descriptions. Farmers driving cattle, sheep and pigs; heavily laden carts of vegetables and grain for the markets; and alongside the road trudged a never-ending stream of men, women and children carrying bundles of goods on their backs. By the time he arrived at Westminster Jack was feeling sore and battered. *I'd rather be stuck on a fishin' boat for a week, goin' over to France, than squeezed into this carriage like a box of smoked mackerel*, he thought.

Jack had been told by Sir William that his accommodation was on the Embankment, near to London Bridge. Crowds of ragged children besieged the coach as it came to a halt, each child vying desperately to get the attention of the weary travellers with the offer of carrying bags, finding a hackney carriage or by directing visitors to London to their lodging houses. Jack ignored them, knowing instinctively that he would be safer finding his own way. The pavements bustled with people hurrying in different directions, avoiding each other's eyes. Smart hackney carriages rattled past and horses jostled at every intersection.

"Am I on the right road for The Angel?" Jack asked a man selling whelks off a wooden barrow.

"No bloody angels round here, mate. Clear off if you don't want to buy anythin'. I get damn fed up with people asking me the way to places."

Sod you, Jack thought. He knew that Westminster was close to the river and after a few missed turnings found himself on the Embankment. A casual wave from a hurrying figure indicated the way to London Bridge and Jack walked on until the lights of a public house with The Angel sign hanging over the gables came into view.

The landlord, Mr Toaster, greeted him civilly enough and warmed considerably when Jack said he was on government business for Sir William Pole.

"Would you like some hot water for a spruce up before eating, Mr Rattenbury?"

Greasy crawler, thought Jack, but said, "Yes, I would welcome that."

A light tap on the door signalled the maid carrying a large jug of hot water. *I could get used to this kind of service,* he thought, ogling the pretty servant girl and looking around his comfortable room.

The rest of the day passed pleasantly enough. Jack wandered around the docks, gazing with pleasure at the three-masted schooners moored alongside wharves laden with goods. *What a wonderful sight,* he marvelled. Standing above London Bridge he watched, fascinated, as the lighters, barges and ferries carried passengers and freight upstream. A constant hubbub of ships' bells and the shouts of dockers rose from the river. As the evening drew in, he walked on up to the Palace of Westminster. The spires of the great building stretched skywards, piercing the evening twilight. Towering arched windows, glowing with candlelight, gave the palace a sense of separation from the earth, as if floating above the

Thames like a vision. Jack could hardly believe his eyes, or his luck. *I shall be in there tomorrow*, he thought, *as an invited guest of Lord Rolle.* A bit different to bein' a guest of His Majesty's prison, like on the last visit.

Jack was not easily awed by wealth and power. It was as alien to his life as the planets, but the scale and richness of the buildings impressed him deeply. Carriage after carriage swept past ferrying men and women dressed in their finest apparel. *So this is where the bolts of silk, lace and embroidered shawls I smuggle back from France and Spain end up,* Jack thought, and smiled with self-congratulation, savouring his links with the scene before him.

The next morning Jack woke early, despite having slept poorly. Used to the quiet of a Devon village, he had been disturbed by the noise of the city. For most of the night the tap room of The Angel had been full of Russian sailors from Mermansk, so he had been told by Mr Toaster. They didn't intend sleeping and spent the night drinking and brawling with doxies, whose shrieking laughter became more desperate and shrill as the night wore on.

A government clerk called Salter arrived at seven o'clock to escort Jack to the House of Lords, and after a good breakfast the two men made their way up the embankment towards Westminster.

"And what do you make of London, Mr Rattenbury?" said the clerk.

"A very fine city, Mr Salter, but in small doses. I'm used to the open sea and clean air. Too many odours for my fancy." Jack was determined not to be subdued by a man who spent his life scribbling on bits of paper and carrying messages.

"Quite, Mr Rattenbury." He made no other attempt to communicate with a man so obviously unable to appreciate city life.

They were met in Westminster Hall by a smart young engineer from the Western Canal Office. "I believe you are here to see Lord Rolle," he said, and set off at a brisk pace through a maze of corridors.

I hope he sticks with me, thought Jack, *I'd never find my way back out of this rabbit warren.*

Lord Rolle's office was small and cramped, with files and plans scattered over every surface. It did, however, have an excellent view out over the river. He jumped to his feet when Jack was shown through the door by the young engineer.

"Good morning, Mr Rattenbury. I trust you had a good journey up from Devonshire?"

The last time Jack had set eyes on Lord Rolle was in Beer, shortly after the Dragoons had left, and that was six or so years back.

"Can't complain, your Lordship, although my preferred method of travel is by boat, as you well know. That way you can guarantee some good fresh air and space to breathe."

"Not much fresh air around Westminster, Mr Rattenbury, but quite a sufficiency of hot air, I believe." He laughed, pleased with his witticism.

"The people here want to pick your brains, Mr Rattenbury. I told them you knew the East Devon coast like the back of your hand and would be the best person to ask for details, which may well not be on any chart. For this service we will pay you one guinea a day, with all your expenses paid. I trust this is satisfactory?"

"I am very grateful, sir, and will do my best to help your lordship," said Jack, hardly able to believe his luck.

A clerk took Jack into a chamber where he met several Counsellors and a gentleman called Sir Isaac Coffin.

"Would you mind telling us, Mr Rattenbury, what trade you follow?"

"Well, sir, it's sometimes fishing, sometimes piloting an' sometimes smuggling. It depends on what comes my way. With a large family to feed I can't be too fussy."

Sir Isaac pressed his plump fingertips together and suppressed a smirk. "Then I imagine you are used to spending a lot of your time plumbing the depth of the sea at various points of the bay from Portland to Start Point."

"That is quite right, sir."

"Can you tell me, Mr Rattenbury, how you would sail a vessel around Portland Bill in a gale blowing south-south-west?"

"Well, if I had the choice, sir, I'd prefer not to be sailing at all under them conditions, an' there be a lot to take into consideration. If it's spring or neap tides, the state of the tide or a foul tide – that is, running in the opposite direction to the wind – all these things would influence my decision. An' also the type of boat an' her loading. If a skipper was sailing from west to east, say, he'd have to get his craft five to seven miles off the race, that is the current running off the Bill. A rough and wet ride, but he could do it. But if he was sailing from east to west, in a gale blowin' south-south-west, then it wouldn't be possible. I wouldn't do it, sir, an' I've bin sailing around the Bill all my workin' life. I'd seek shelter in Weymouth. In my opinion, there's no possibility of a ship getting round the Bill under them conditions."

"Have you seen many vessels lost through not having a safe harbour, Mr Rattenbury?"

"I have, sir, many indeed."

The questions continued throughout the day, with a break for lunch, when Jack was left to fend for himself. On their return, the members, having enjoyed a large meal complemented by excellent French wine, were in good humour. Sir Isaac sat back in his studded leather armchair looking satisfied.

"You lead a dangerous life, Mr Rattenbury, one that is often led outside the laws of our country. But I have heard from my good friend Lord Rolle that you are generous with your booty."

Jack watched Sir Isaac with the intensity of a man watching a snake, not quite sure in which direction the conversation was leading. "Well, sir," he said confidently, "there's many a gentleman who has benefited from my endeavours."

"Quite so, quite so, Mr Rattenbury. That will be all today. I would thank you for your considered opinions and request you return to London in two weeks' time, when we will have further questions to put to you."

Jack left Westminster with the distinct impression that it would be wise to watch your back and your words in such a place. He walked down the Embankment towards The Angel but this time gave up all thought of sleep and spent the night drinking with the crew of a revenue cutter, in harbour for repair. The talk ranged over their work chasing smugglers, mainly from the Kent area. "They're scum," declared one officer loudly. "Transportation's the best solution, just get 'em out of the country. They'd run a knife through a man, an' not think twice about it."

Jack smiled to himself but wisely stayed silent.

The following morning he went to the agent's office to collect his money and by twelve noon was on the coach heading for the south-west.

Hannah, Frances and Anne were agog to hear Jack's tales of London.

"I would love to go there, Jack, to see the clothes an' the palaces. I've been told they have gas lights in the streets. Did you see any?"

Jack nodded. "They help to find your way round the streets but the best of it was The Angel. Big joints of beef and as much ale as you could put away. I met these sailors from Mermansk and the stories they had to tell, you wouldn't believe. They'd bin stuck in London all the winter 'cause their home ports was froze over. Didn't look as if they cared, mind you. But yes, I did see the gas lights an' very handsome they looked."

Will and John were more interested in talking about a run they had planned for the following week. "Let's go down The Dolphin, Father, we could do with a jar."

Most people in the village had heard that Jack had been called to Westminster and his mates were eager to hear his news. When he walked into the bar with William and John he was welcomed like a returning hero. "I bet you sold them a yarn, Jack," said Joe Stoker, slapping Jack on the back.

"One thing I didn't like the sound of, Joe, they is talkin' about putting a harbour in Beer. Wouldn't be long before they had a cutter moored there."

There was a lull in the banter. "We'd find a way of givin' them a run for their money, don' you worry about that," said Alan Westlake. "They'd wish they'd never set eyes on us."

Eventually William pulled his father away from the bar. "Don't get stuck in there, Father, we've got things to talk about." Jack listened to the plans they had for picking up twenty kegs in Cherbourg, but found that his attention kept wandering back to what had taken place in London over the past week.

"Abe Mutter's helped us a lot while you were inside," said John, determined to hold his father's attention. "Mostly his runs have worked out, so this one should be sound."

"That's all right by me, son," said Jack, now feeling the effects of a large brandy and several pints of ale. He was enjoying himself and well into his cups. "Abe's a good friend to our family an' always around to give a helping hand when it's needed. Let's drink on that, me boys. When do we go?"

Unnoticed by Jack and the regulars, who were busy celebrating his return, Albert Rankin was sitting in the snug listening to every word.

"Friday night's the best," said John. "There's no moon and the tide's right."

The Cherbourg run went well enough and Jack revelled in the wind scouring his face and watching the open sea part before the bow. "Freedom, Will, you only knows how precious it is when you've lost it. No more bloody prisons for me."

But the return trip did not go to plan. As they were set to turn for Beer Roads, a cutter called *The Invincible* ran in fast from the south-east. Jack, William and John met Abe that night with a tale of woe. "The buggers must have been lying low just off Lyme and watched us coming in. They would not give up and chased us till dark. In the end we had to sink the kegs off Eype beach and make a run for home," said William. "John went back out the next day under guise of a fishin' trip, an' had to watch as they was neatly picked up by the cutter."

"Some goddamned maggot informed on us and if I find out who it was they'll get chucked over the cliff," snarled William. "There's no such a villain as him who informs on his own, an' they deserve all they get."

A couple of months passed and Jack was beginning to think that Lord Rolle had forgotten his promises, or that his plans for the ship canal had been abandoned, but late one afternoon there was a knock on the door.

"Come in," called Hannah. "It's Daniel, isn't it, from Shute House?"

The boy pulled off his cap and smiled shyly at Hannah. "I have a message from Sir William for Mr Rattenbury. Would he please proceed to the House of Lords as soon as he is able."

Jack grinned and pulled Daniel up to the table. "I think you should have a drink before going back up to Shute. What's your name again?"

"Daniel," said the boy clearly. He could be no more than eight years old.

"Well try this, Daniel," said Hannah and put a small mug of watered-down cider on the table.

"Good news," said Jack, rubbing his hands. "You can tell Sir William that I will be in London within two days, an' here's a farthin' for your trouble."

This time Jack had had more warning, so he made sure he was well scrubbed up and wearing some decent clothes. Hannah laid out a linen shirt and a black serge jacket, usually kept for funerals. The britches were none too smart, but his boots took on a good shine after a liberal rub of goose fat.

Jack tied his hair back with a ribbon and looked in the mirror. "Not so bad for an old sea dog, eh, Hannah?"

Hannah smiled indulgently at Jack's vanity.

Ann was watching her father's efforts to smarten himself up with some amusement. "Bring us some new ribbons, Father," she said cheekily. She was now twelve and constantly primping and brushing her long black hair. Anne quickly shushed her into silence.

This time Jack caught the mail coach in Honiton. His spirits rose as he saw the horses pull into the yard of the Golden Lion, steam ballooning from their nostrils after the pull up from Exeter. The Post Office took great pride in maintaining their coaches, which bore a distinctive maroon and black livery. The names of the towns at either end of the journey were painted on the doors, in this case Exeter to London.

Jack climbed aboard; on this journey he had decided to sit behind the coachman and not suffer the stifling fug created by the carriage passengers. As on the previous trip, he stopped overnight in Reading and reached London by eleven the following morning.

Jack went straight to The Angel and this time was received like royalty.

"Mr Rattenbury, good to see you again," said the landlord, clapping him on the back. "We have the best room in the inn ready for you," he said, rubbing his hands. And your supper, what is your fancy? We have a good plump chicken in the oven, or maybe you would prefer some roast beef."

"The roast beef will do me fine, Mr Toaster, just fine."

Jack settled down to a very comfortable evening, greatly entertained by the landlord's tales of visiting seamen. "All colours and creeds, Mr Rattenbury, they come from all over the world to The Pool of London. Mark you, it's wise to watch your pockets as some of 'em have got nimble fingers. Them Russians left two weeks after you, an' I was glad to see the back of 'em."

The following morning Jack walked down the Embankment towards Westminster feeling confident and delighted with his good fortune. He had been told to proceed to Westminster Hall at ten o'clock, where Lord Rolle and Dr Palmer would be waiting.

The magnificent vaulted hall was full of people all going about their business, none taking the slightest notice of a man standing quietly, watching the throng. Jack was gripped by the scene around him. There were few women, but elderly men in wigs and flowing red capes, edged in gold and ermine, walked along the corridors looking haughty and unapproachable. Small groups of party members stood in animated discussion. Jack edged nearer.

"What you have to remember, sir," said a young man, obviously intent on impressing his peers, "is that we already have two thousand two hundred miles of canals in this country, and there is no place in England, south of Durham, further than fifteen miles from water communication. This must be the way forward; roads are too costly and in constant need of repair." His peers nodded and continued in animated debate on the advantages and possible disadvantages of canal transportation.

Amidst this scene Lord Rolle and Dr Palmer emerged, the doctor looking somewhat less colourful in a brown double-breasted dress coat and matching trousers. "Mr Rattenbury, so sorry to keep you waiting, please come through. This will be a somewhat more formal affair than on your last visit and you will be obliged to swear on oath before we proceed."

"That's all right by me, sir," said Jack. "I've nothin' to hide on this occasion."

Jack stood on a slightly raised platform and placed his hand on the Bible.

"Repeat this after me," said the Committee Clerk, and carefully read Jack the oath as if addressing a five-year-old. Jack stifled a grin. *If he but knew it, I could repeat that oath off the top of my head, no trouble at all*, he thought.

"I swear by almighty God to tell the truth, the whole truth, an' nothin' but the truth, so help me God," said Jack in a clear and confident tone.

"Please take a seat, Mr Rattenbury," said Lord Rolle smiling encouragingly.

The questions on this occasion were more specific and detailed, ranging from the effect of tides on shipping, to how the shoreline had changed over the past thirty years or so. The Committee sat in rooms which appeared small and plain in comparison to the huge ornate chamber of the House of Lords. Ancient oak panels lined the walls and the ceilings were dark from the smoke of oil lamps. One glance at the gathering singled Jack out as a man lacking in formal education and wealth, but if Jack sensed this at all it made little difference to his demeanour. Far from being intimidated, he rose to the occasion and graphically informed the Committee, digging deep into his wealth of knowledge in relation to sea and shore conditions. His quick wit and good humour was a welcome relief from the tedium of technical seamanship.

Jack attended the Committee daily and could see that a canal and harbour would totally change life for the inhabitants of Beer. He listened avidly to the arguments, both for and against. By day three he had become enthused by the idea of a ship canal connecting the Bristol and English Channels. The harbour was another matter, however, and he, understandably maybe, retained serious misgivings because of the effect this would have on his livelihood.

Chapter 22

As the days passed, Jack was unaware that he had attracted the attention of a lady who visited the House on a daily basis in connection with her interest in geology.

He doesn't strike me like the usual stuffed shirts found around here, she thought, watching Jack make his way through the crowds to the upper end of Westminster Hall in the company of Dr Palmer. *I like the way he walks on the balls of his feet, slightly bouncy, and looking like he couldn't give tuppence for what people think of him.*

Each morning she attempted to cross Jack's path before he reached Dr Palmer, a man she had met briefly on one occasion during a visit to Colyton. Days passed while she considered an acceptable approach, unwilling to risk arousing the doctor's suspicions, and fearful of a rejection from the man to whom she was now strongly attracted. *It's tomorrow or never,* she thought.

The following morning she dressed carefully, giving extra attention to her soft blond hair, which had the unfortunate tendency to fly in all directions. She chose pretty but practical clothing and smoothed lavender cologne over her neck and shoulders. On her head she pinned a blue bonnet, edged with tiny silk flowers. She arrived early and stood near the entrance of the great hall, where she had observed the two men meeting for the past two weeks.

Jack arrived early and the woman watched him for a while before spotting the doctor making his way across the crowded hall. "Good morning, Dr Palmer," she called, affecting an air of delighted surprise. "Mrs Daisy Morrison," she said, holding out her hand. "We have met before when I visited Colyton with my husband. He gave a talk on the geology of the Lyme Bay coastline, if you remember."

"Good morning to you, Mrs Morrison. Of course I remember. And what brings you to Westminster?"

"You may not be aware, Dr Palmer, but I am also greatly interested in the geology of the coastline around Lyme and I wish to know the effect, if any, that the planned sea defences may have on the shoreline."

"By coincidence, Mrs Morrison, the Lords are also engaged in some quite extensive discussions in relation to that area. We have engaged Mr Rattenbury, a native of Beer, to give us his expert opinion on the sea and shoreline conditions in Lyme Bay and, in particular, the Beer and Seaton area," Dr Palmer turned to Jack. "May I introduce you to Mrs Daisy Morrison."

Jack extended his hand and inclined his head.

"I have visited Lyme on many occasions, Mr Rattenbury. Are you familiar with the town?"

Jack stumbled slightly over his words but recovered quickly. "You could say, Mrs Morrison, that I am virtually a native of Lyme, a town very close to my heart."

Jack smiled directly into her face and to his amusement she did not look away but quite brazenly smiled back, her eyes sparkling.

"I search for fossils on the beach with a lady called Mary Anning. Have you heard of her?"

"No, ma'am, can't say that I have, but I would like to hear more about your interest in Lyme Bay."

Daisy could see that if she didn't make a move Jack would be ushered away by Dr Palmer. "When will you be returning to Devon, Mr Rattenbury?"

Before Jack could answer, Dr Palmer turned briskly and put his hand on Jack's shoulder. "We must be off, Mrs Morrison, the Committee is waiting to hear from our good friend here. Good day to you."

"I am here till the end of this week, ma'am," said Jack, refusing to be rushed, "when I shall be returning to Devon on the Honiton coach."

Mrs Morrison put out her hand to say goodbye, and to Jack's surprise. smoothly passed a tiny card into his palm.

Jack spent the rest of the day poring over charts and explaining the difficulties, which he frequently encountered while manoeuvring boats in and out of Lyme Bay. What he didn't mention was the Excise cutters, which were the bane of his life.

At last the questioning came to an end, and Lord Rolle indicated that Jack was free to leave. "Please attend tomorrow, Mr Rattenbury. Your knowledge is invaluable."

Jack left Westminster feeling pleased with the day but aware that, if he chose, the night could offer an entirely different experience. He returned to The Angel for a meal, and with the intention of asking the landlord to look at the card. Mr Toaster studied the gilt-edged card closely and noted that it was written in a woman's handwriting.

"An address in Knightsbridge," he said, looking puzzled. "This is an entirely new area to me, Mr Rattenbury, but I think you'll find it's north of the river, all new houses being built there, so somebody told me. Best thing you can do is take a hackney carriage." The landlord looked at Jack curiously, but held his tongue. No doubt he would hear more about it before the week was out.

"Beef again, Mr Rattenbury?" he asked, returning to business. "We've a lovely piece of brisket on the bone, if it takes your fancy. You may care to take a walk up round where the government plan to build Trafalgar Square this evening. It's being made better, more grand you know, to commemorate Lord Nelson and his victory at Trafalgar. Where this country would be without its seamen I don't know."

Jack let the landlord chatter on and agreed wholeheartedly, but maybe not with the same patriotic fervour. After finishing his meal and treating himself to another glass of port wine, Jack left The Angel and walked along the Embankment.

London appalled and fascinated Jack. He was unused to the press of people, unfamiliar with streets full of faceless hurrying multitudes, who neither knew nor cared who you were or where you were going. Leaving the river, he made his way up towards The Strand, marvelling at the imposing dressed-stone buildings which towered over the scurrying pedestrians. But the alleyways told another story. Human waste ran in gullies and the crumbling, rat-infested tenements teemed with filthy children dressed in nothing but rags. *I know that Beer can smell a bit strong when the brook gets clogged up,* thought Jack, *'but by God, it's nothin' to the stink of this place.*

Jack had been told by Mr Toaster to turn left on reaching The Strand and after walking for a while he could hear a sound he recognised from Beer quarries. The tac, tac, tac of a hundred masons' hammers filled the air. Men squatted, heads bent over huge blocks of stone, shaping and smoothing. Not one would stop long enough to answer Jack's questions. "That looks like Dartmoor granite to me," he said to a man covered in dust.

"It's going to be some sort of column, that's all I know," grunted one. "But yes, I think you're right, a place called Foggin Tor."

Jack smiled. After watching the masons for a while he followed the lane going northwards, past the church of St Martin-in-the-Fields, starkly outlined against the evening sky. As he walked he pondered again on the abrupt unfriendly natives of London. *Nobody's got time for you here, unless you're spending money.* But very quickly he was distracted by the changing scene around him. *It's like another country,* he thought and stared in amazement at groups of immigrants from Europe and beyond. They had colonised a sprawling area called Soho. Strange cooking smells rose up from wood fires. There were few houses as such, and whole families lived in rough shelters made of tarred sacking. Each group somehow managed to retain their individual nationality, often through music. Jack listened to the haunting strains of a violin played by an old man dressed in a long black coat. He was physically frail, and his thin, deeply lined face traced the suffering he had endured. But the music somehow bore the weight of his sadness. As he played his foot tapped out a rhythm and his eyes sparkled with pleasure.

Despite the appalling poverty Jack sensed a hum of energy. He felt no threat from the people there and wandered around the encampment and listened curiously to men engaged in animated discussion, sad that he couldn't understand a word.

The card lay in his pocket like a hot coal. No matter how far he wandered or how interesting the scene around him became, it remained an insistent reminder of Mrs Morrison.

"Have you heard of Knightsbridge?" Jack asked a young man wearing a black peaked cap. He was met with a blank stare and hands raised in bemused incomprehension.

The night was now drawing in and Jack turned to thread his way back along the narrow paths and alleyways. Eventually he found himself on a main thoroughfare opposite St Ann's Church, alongside which was a coach stand.

"I'm tryin' to find my way to Montpelier Walk in Knightsbridge, sir. Is it too far for me to walk?"

One look at Jack told the coachman that he was not a city man and certainly unfamiliar with the streets of London. "It's bloody miles, mate, but I'll take you there for a shilling."

Jack knew that he was probably paying through the nose but the card in his pocket was not to be ignored. As the coachman pulled away he snapped the whip over the horses' heads until they settled into a steady trot. The teeming streets soon opened out into parkland and after twenty minutes the carriage pulled up on the edge of a broad street lined with newly planted poplar trees. Through the gloom Jack could just see the end of a curving terrace of new houses, each with steps leading up to the front door.

"This is where you're looking for, sir," said the driver and held out his hand for the fare. Jack paid up grudgingly; it seemed an extortionate sum for such a short distance.

After the tap of horses' hooves had faded, Jack walked slowly around the crescent while he considered what to do next. The houses looked rather grand, but as if drawn by a magnet he walked towards the end house. "I know it's number fifteen," he muttered, having been told this by Mr Toaster. At last he found a number which matched the address on the card. The street was quite dark, the only light came from the windows of houses which were occupied; the others looked dark and hollow, not quite finished. Jack went up the steps two at a time and, before waiting to think, rang the bell. The chimes echoed back through the door, deep and rich.

What am I doing here? he thought. *If I'm not careful I'll get a thick ear from her husband.* But it was too late.

Mrs Morrison opened the door, looking radiant. "Mr Rattenbury, how kind of you to come."

She stood framed in the doorway, the warm glow of the hall lamps illuminating her pale blond hair. A blue dress of soft muslin swathed her shoulders in delicate folds. Gone were the sensible brogues, demure woollen skirt and tailored cotton blouse.

Jack stood very still, for once in his life at a loss for words. Mrs Morrison looked past Jack into the night. The newly paved street was deserted but she was quite obviously at pains to get him into the house and off the doorstep.

"Come in, do please come in. I have been waiting for you," she said, and reached out her hand.

Every nerve in Jack's body felt taut and stretched. He ached to reach out and touch her, to gently slip the featherlight muslin from her creamy shoulders. Cautiously he stepped over the doorway and into the hall. The house felt quite empty but Jack could see into the drawing room where a fire blazed, throwing shadows around the bare walls.

"I don't bite, Mr Rattenbury," said Mrs Morrison, laughing.

Jack smiled and walked on into the drawing room. A large painting hung over the fireplace of a man dressed in a black frock coat, an academic gown draped over his shoulders. His face was finely drawn and somewhat severe; the eyes stared coldly into Jack's curious gaze. "Is this your father, Mrs Morrison?" Jack asked.

She turned away and laughed but left Jack no wiser. "Would you care for a brandy, Mr Rattenbury?"

Jack nodded and made an effort to relax. "An' where do you get your brandy, Mrs Morrison?" He watched her every movement, not yet sure of her intentions and not wanting anything to disrupt the delicate web of promise she was weaving around him.

"Call me Daisy, won't you? Mrs Morrison is never a name that suits me, I feel.

Jack looked into her clear blue eyes and felt the smooth French brandy spreading its warm glow.

"The brandy was a present from Lord Rolle to my husband," said Daisy, and for separate reasons, known only to themselves, they laughed long and loud. The evening passed all too quickly while Jack entertained Daisy with tales of foreign shores and the many adventures he had survived. But neither could or wanted to ignore the intense attraction each had for the other. Jack felt intoxicated with her smell, her softness and the way she smiled, luring him towards her.

"You're a bit of a mystery, Daisy," he said, wanting to test the waters and discover just what was on offer.

"That may be so, Jack, but you're no mystery to me," she said softly, and ran her fingers across his lips.

Neither could remember how they'd reached the bedroom but for both of them the dawn came much too soon.

The next morning Jack lay in bed luxuriating in the crisp linen sheets while Daisy looked at him appreciatively. His broad chest, covered in a mat of dark curly hair, was set in stark relief against the delicate femininity of the room. The walls were painted a soft peach and diaphanous white curtains drifted in front of the large windows. A woman's room, which held no scent or stamp of masculinity.

"You're a fine one, Daisy. What does your husband make of all this?"

"My husband is very seldom here. In fact he is in Lyme this very moment doing a geological survey of the coast. But tell me more about yourself," said Daisy, who seemed to have an insatiable curiosity about Jack's life.

"I wouldn't know where to start," said Jack. "Although I'm ashamed to say it lying here, I've got a good wife and five children at home. You can't imagine a more different life to your own. The Committee in Westminster asked me what work I do, so I said, fishing, piloting and smuggling. But if I'm honest, mostly it's smuggling. An' I don't make any apologies for it."

Daisy looked at Jack fondly. *He's not a handsome man,* she thought, *but he has more life in his little finger than my husband has in his whole body.*

"You have no reason to apologise to me, Jack. I am well aware of how hard life is for fishermen and the reason they engage in smuggling is out of need rather than greed. I don't doubt that if I were a man I would join you. Smuggling must be an exciting business to be in."

Jack laughed. "You've certainly got the nerve for it, Daisy, but it's a bloody hard life and I wouldn't wish it on a lady like yourself. I've spent more months looking at prison walls than I would like."

"Sometimes when I'm on the beach with Mary Anning searching for fossils, we come across kegs that have been washed ashore. Mary is a very good woman and sympathetic to the poorer people in Lyme. She hides the kegs under rocks and let's people who need the money know where they are."

"Well, I expect they're grateful for that, Daisy, there's not many around who looks out for their welfare. But I must be off," said Jack reluctantly. "Lord Rolle is expecting me at eight o'clock."

Daisy lay back, laughing. "You look like the cat that got the cream."

"That's just how I feel," said Jack, sounding bemused. "These last two weeks have been some of the most amazin' of my life, an' that's saying something."

Jack looked at her smooth young body. All of him wanted to stay, but after a last lingering kiss he left to find a carriage for the ride back to Westminster.

Jack's last day before the Committee was filled with detailed discussions in relation to the planned harbour for Beer. He could now visualise the full extent of the development and his mind boggled at the impact such a huge structural change would have on the tiny tucked-away cove. Little did the Committee members realise, or care, that, should their plans come to fruition, it would change Jack's life profoundly, and the life of the people in Beer beyond recognition.

Lord Rolle shook Jack's hand warmly when the hearing ended after a long day. "Please call at my house in Grosvenor Square before you leave tonight, Mr Rattenbury. You will find yourself well rewarded for the information you have provided the committee over the past two weeks."

Later that evening Jack walked up to Grosvenor Square, savouring his last evening in London. He knocked at the door of Lord Rolle's large house and was welcomed by his secretary, a small neat man dressed in a well-tailored frock coat. "This includes all your expenses, Mr Rattenbury, and his Lordship asked me to put in a little extra. The sum total amounts to twenty guineas. Please put your mark here," he said, presenting Jack with a leather-bound accounts ledger.

The coach left Westminster at four o'clock the following morning en route for Reading. Jack had enjoyed his last evening in London, wandering around the streets with money in his pocket. He bought ribbons for the girls and something special for Hannah, a flowered bonnet. For his mother he found a warm woollen shawl. Jack had hours to mull over the last two weeks as the coach jerked and bumped over the rutted roads. *It's been bloody amazin', like visiting another world altogether*, he thought. *But I'll have to keep the best bit under my hat. What Hannah don't know won't hurt her.*

Chapter 23

The next seven years passed swiftly, with the addition of two more daughters in the Rattenbury family, named Elizabeth and Ruth. The last child had been named Ruth after her maternal grandmother and at the age of forty-seven Hannah sincerely hoped that this would be her last experience of childbirth.

William was now married to a Beer girl called Susannah Pike. The couple lived with their three children in a small thatched cottage in Fore Street, rented from Lord Rolle. Marriage and fatherhood had not subdued William and as the years passed his true nature emerged. A superficial meeting could give the impression that he had inherited his father's flamboyant personality, but there was one quite significant difference between them. William lacked his father's charm, and had become notorious along the coast for his ruthless and violent behaviour. This dark side of his nature was further incited by Susannah, who was very ambitious and actively encouraged her husband's smuggling activities. The young girl who had attracted William with her inky black flowing hair and strong shapely body had now become bloated and coarse, paying little attention to her appearance. The couple fought like cat and dog and rarely did a Saturday night go by without a furious row erupting after an evening in The Dolphin. A regular cause for argument was Susannah's attempts to make William account for every penny entering or leaving the house. He now ran two luggers off Beer beach and Susannah was set on acquiring a sloop she had spotted for sale in Lyme. Each week she counted the money which she kept in a leather pouch hidden under a flagstone in the kitchen.

"How many runs have you done this month? I've been counting it up and there's some missin', William. Have you bin' givin' money to your mother again?"

William would shift uneasily under this interrogation. "That's between me and my mother," he'd snap, "so keep your bloody nose out of it, woman."

Susannah knew that one more word from her and William would erupt and fists would fly, so she'd bite her lip and bide her time. But William knew he'd not heard the end of it, and always strove to have the last word on the matter. "My mother's had a hard life one way and another and if I can make it any easier I damn well will," he'd shout angrily, pounding the table with his clenched fist.

Susannah was intensely jealous of William's relationship with his mother. He made no secret of the fact that he adored her, and Susannah, although not noted for her sensitivity, knew that she had to step carefully.

Jack was now well over fifty years of age and apart from episodes of gout he remained hale and hearty. He had not bought another boat since the loss of the *Elizabeth and Kitty* and earned his money working out of Lyme, delivering cargo. When back in Beer, he more often than not worked with William on contraband runs between Devon and Cherbourg. But free trading was becoming more difficult with each passing year. The Government was engaged in a fierce and determined battle to bring an end to smuggling, and a service which combined the Navy and the Customs, henceforth called the Coastguard, was formed. The new service gave Jack far less room to manoeuvre. Severe prison sentences were meted out to any smugglers caught with sufficient evidence to procure a prosecution, and anyone caught in the near vicinity of a smuggling run was under suspicion. The new service quickly became expert at gathering intelligence, and extensive records were kept on individuals along the coast with a history of smuggling.

Despite the growing danger and harassment, Jack and his sons continued to bring in contraband goods whenever the opportunity arose. But relations did not always run smoothly between the brothers. William and John, in particular, were often at daggers drawn and Jack was at great pains to keep them from engaging in a constant battle. Abraham was now sixteen and already an experienced seaman. He was of a more affable nature, and out of the brothers more closely resembled Jack in his easy charm and good nature.

One night after a rough but successful run to Alderney, Jack, William and John were gathered at William's house, with the intention of dividing the spoils, when Susannah looked over John's shoulder and accused him of taking too large a cut.

"It's William's boat, you got to remember that," she said, her voice shrill and hectoring. "He should get the bigger part of any run when it's his boat you're usin'." John jumped up from the table and pushed Susannah hard against the wall, but true to form she came back at him with her fists up.

"Keep this bloody wife of yours in order, William, I don't fight with women."

But Susannah was not to be silenced and continued to shout and demand that John hand over a quarter of what he rightly considered to be his share.

Jack stayed silent. These confrontations had occurred many times before and he knew that diplomacy was the only method of preventing a major eruption. "Come on, lads," he said, trying to inject a more light-hearted tone into the proceedings. "We can sort this out without any bloodshed". But it was as if he had not spoken and the atmosphere in the tiny room remained ugly and charged with impending violence. Susannah could barely conceal her fury and continued to rant and complain.

"Here, take this," said William, arrogantly throwing John's money on the table.

But for John this violent confrontation was the final straw, and without a word he gathered up his dues and left his brother's house, slamming the door behind him. The following morning, after quietly saying goodbye to his grandmother, he walked to Lyme where he boarded a fishing boat heading for Brixham. *I'll make for Scotland,* he thought. *I did well there with father and Abe when we was working off the north-west coast. Freezing cold, but the money was good.*

Anne was distraught to see John leave and knew in her heart that she was unlikely ever to see him again.

In November 1832, Jack was again before Exeter Court with his son William and two other Beer men, a labourer William Abbot and a fisherman by the name of Isaac Lane. Giving evidence, Jack claimed that at seven o'clock on the evening of the 19th November his vessel had been chased by Lieutenant Buxton, Chief Officer of the Beer Coastguard Station. He no longer cut a robust, swaggering figure in the dock. His hair was thin, and he walked with a marked limp, owing to the effects of gout over the years. But he held his head high, determined to defend himself.

"Your Honour, when Lieutenant Buxton came aboard I explained that we was fishin' in the bay and if he would care to look over our vessel he would find nothin' to incriminate us with. His men hove the grappling irons overboard to no purpose, but still we was taken into custody. All they found was a piece of rope, about one fathom in length."

The elderly judge listened carefully to this unlikely plea of innocence, his chin cupped in the palm of his hand. He had followed Jack's career with interest over the years and more than once had been rewarded for his leniency with a few kegs.

For this trial Jack had employed two attorneys, apparently of the opinion that, as so little evidence could be brought, they stood a good chance of the case being dismissed. But a few years had passed since Jack had last been in a Court of Law and in the meantime he had failed to understand that, despite not being caught, his activities were closely monitored by the Coastguard. They now held an extensive dossier of information, sufficient to convince the authorities that he was still involved in smuggling.

The trial lasted for six hours and with no hard evidence, other than the piece of rope, Jack was committed to prison, along with his two companions. William was carried to a naval flagship at Plymouth to be impressed, but there he was found to be unfit for naval service and within a week joined Jack in Dorchester Gaol.

"I'm getting to old for this lark," Jack grumbled to anyone who would listen. He was kept apart from William on account of his reputation for escaping confinement, usually by the use of his persuasive tongue and wily nature.

"I shouldn't be in here at all on the evidence of a bit of rope. I'm determined to petition the Board for my release," Jack complained bitterly. "This is an unjust conviction and I'll not let up until I get released."

Jack consulted with his attorney and begged him to construct a petition, which would sway the prison board to listen to his appeal for a re-trial or an early release. He was convinced that when this petition was read justice would prevail.

"YourHonorable petitioner, with the greatest contrition for his past faults, does acknowledge the crime for which he now suffers, and do most solemnly promise to your Lordships never more to be guilty of any offence against the Revenue Laws.

Your humble petitioner sheweth that he is a man upwards of 58 years of age and the father of ten children, two of which are afflicted and crippled. They have been supported by your humble petitioner without any assistance from the parish, which I am sorry to say, is now not the case. Your humble petitioner has been confined upwards of eight months and do most humbly implore your Lordship's forgiveness, that I may again be able to return home to a disconsolate wife and an afflicted, helpless family."

Jack Rattenbury.

Weeks and months crawled past. And while, during previous periods of imprisonment Jack would have spent his time planning escape, or working the system to ensure that he improved his lot, he was now unable to summon the strength to fight. Time weighed heavy. Incarcerated in the rotting cesspit of Dorchester Gaol he became obsessed with the unjust nature of his sentence and the winter chill gripped his bones and entered his soul. Each day he asked the guard if any response to his petition had been received.

"They've buried you and thrown away the key," said one. Jack became a source of amusement to the guards who would stand outside his cell and goad him. "Your smugglin' days is over, Rattenbury. What did they call you? Rob Roy of the West." Their mocking laughter would bounce off the walls and into Jack's head, ready to replay endlessly through the long sleepless nights.

Just before Christmas a reply to his petition arrived from Exeter Court.

"Well I never." said the guard sarcastically, "Somebody has remembered you at last."

Jack was called from his cell to appear before the Board and to hear the Governor's response to his plea.

"Mr Rattenbury, in my opinion you are incorrigible. You have been before this Court on numerous occasions over the years and reading this petition I can see that it is nothing but a tissue of lies. I have no doubt, that should you be released, you would within the month be back to your old ways."

Jack opened his mouth to speak but was silenced immediately by the clerk.

"Take this man back to his cell," said the Governor, "and I would call on you, Mr Rattenbury, not to waste my time again."

Jack looked at the fat complacent Governor with the utmost loathing before he was roughly grabbed by the arms and hustled out of the Court.

"Here comes Rob Roy!" shouted one of the guards, when Jack was brought into the gaol yard. "No Christmas pudding for you, Rattenbury."

Jack ignored his tormentors, who were unaware that he had returned from the hearing in an altogether different frame of mind. Anger, that useful fuel, motivated him. *Hypocritical bastard!* he fumed inwardly. *The bloody judges don't turn down their share of good French brandy when it's on offer. There's two rules as far as I can see – one for the rich and one for the poor. Anyway, some of it was true,* he muttered to himself, *I know that Hannah is strugglin' to keep food on the table.*

Through the gaol grapevine Jack heard that William and his two other companions were to be released and this did nothing to lessen the feeling that he was being penalised unfairly. *I'll be out of here in six months or I'll leave in a box*, he thought, but wisely concealed his feelings and turned his energy to achieving his aim.

Hannah could visit Jack only on rare occasions, but as his second Christmas in prison was coming up, she accepted a loan for her coach fare and a night's lodging from William. One morning, a week before Christmas Day she walked up to Hangman's Stone to catch the 6a.m. coach to Dorchester. The journey was a considerable undertaking for Hannah, who rarely left the village. Both her parents were now long dead, taking with them the necessity for her yearly visit to Lyme. The road wound along the coast, full of pot holes and deep ruts, carved by the wheels of heavy farm carts and horses' hooves. On reaching Lyme Regis the coach stopped for half an hour, giving Hannah the opportunity to stretch her legs and walk past her parents' old house. *Still there*, she thought and watched a child playing in the window, much as she had done at a similar age. Suddenly a blast from the coachman's horn broke through her reverie and gave the signal for passengers to return. Hannah hurried back, her mind full of memories and feelings of nostalgia.

"You'll have to walk up the steep bit out of the town," shouted the coachman. "The mud's too deep for the horses to get a grip with a full load."

Hannah picked up her skirts, to avoid the steaming piles of horse dung, and stumbled up the hill in the direction of Charmouth. The coach was waiting at the top of the hill and the passengers climbed thankfully aboard. Progress was slow across the rolling Dorset hills, the carriage swayed and pitched in a most alarming fashion. *This is worse than a lugger in a south-west gale*, thought Hannah, who felt quite faint with nausea.

But the worst of the journey was not over.

"You'll have to get out and push here, ladies and gentlemen," shouted the coachman on reaching Lambert's Hill. A collective groan went up as once again the passengers disembarked. A biting north wind hit Hannah full in the face as she stepped down out of the coach. Thick soupy mud slid up to her ankles and over the top of her boots. Crack, the coachman curled his whip over the heads of the horses, their nostrils flared with effort as they strained to pull the now empty coach up the steep gradient. Passengers young and old floundered, the skirts of the women dragging in the mud as they struggled to stop from falling. Once over the top, they pulled their weary bodies up into the carriage and the horses set off at a brisk trot for the remaining miles into Dorchester. By the time the coach pulled into the yard of The Crown Inn it was pitch black and Hannah was exhausted. She followed her fellow travellers into the tap room where she ordered a glass of mulled wine and sat in front of the blazing log fire to dry her sodden skirts.

After an hour she had attracted the attention of the landlord who came over to enquire if she needed a room for the night. Hannah looked a sorry sight and very much aware that she could be taken for a vagrant. "I'm in Dorchester to visit a relative," she said, but I'm wondering if I should stay here the night as it's now too dark for me to find her house, which I believe is on the outskirts of town. What do you charge for your cheapest room?"

"By rights we are full tonight, ma'am, but I have one, the size of a cupboard, in the roof which you can have for a shilling."

Hannah gratefully accepted this offer and found that she could afford a plate of meat and potatoes. The wine worked its magic and with a pleasantly full stomach she made her way up to 'the cupboard' and was asleep before her head touched the rock-hard pillow.

The following morning Hannah woke feeling refreshed and eager to see Jack. She washed her hands and face in a bowl of icy water and after brushing and tying her hair into a knot at the back of her head she set off. Hannah could not find the courage to ask the landlord directions to the gaol but walked down the main street and asked the first woman she met.

"It's about a mile down this road, my dear. You need to go straight on down to the outskirts of the town and the gaol is on a hillside. You can't miss it."

Hannah followed the woman's directions and after half an hour found herself looking at the long drive which lead up to the prison gate. Beside the gate hung a gibbet and she was grateful that, at least for today, no poor figure was hanging from it. *Come on, girl,* Hannah chivvied herself. *No time to get windy.* She gave the bell an energetic pull and waited. At last a small side door opened and a guard looked at her suspiciously. "I'm here to visit my husband, Jack Rattenbury," she said clearly, making sure to keep her head up and shoulders back. The guard closed the door without a word.

Hannah waited for twenty minutes or more before the door opened again and the guard motioned for her to enter. A shudder went down Hannah's back as the door clanged behind her and the cold grey prison walls formed an impenetrable barrier to every gift life had to offer. The guard led her to a small room and quite soon Jack was brought in, heavily manacled.

The couple sat either side of a wooden table in silence until Jack found the first question. "Are you all right, Hannah?"

Hannah laughed softly. "Of course I'm all right, Jack, but the same can't be said of you, my dear."

With that the floodgates opened, and Jack fired questions at Hannah like a man dying of thirst. "How's our Frances and Ann gettin' on? It's terrible in here, Hannah. All I have to do is sit around and worry. Even when they give us work it doesn't stop. If I'm not worrying about you, it's mother or Frances. Just like a torture, it doesn't stop."

Hannah could see that Jack's state of mind was disturbed. This was unusual. "I know it's horrible in here, Jack, but you can usually put up with it. What's different this time?"

Jack sighed. "I can't get it out of my mind, Hannah, that this sentence is unjust. They put me in here with no evidence against me. They've already let our William and the other two out, so why do I have to stay here? I feel buried alive. I'm desperate to get out of this place and have thought over who could put in a good word for me with the Governor. What do you think about contacting Colonel William Pinny, the M.P. for Lyme? He was a good friend of your father. They won't take any notice of my pleas but they may listen to him."

"That may well work, Jack," said Hannah thoughtfully. "Just leave it to me. I know that father was not always sympathetic towards you, but I'm sure, if he was still with us, he would agree that you have done your time. But listen, I don't want to leave before tellin' you some good news. Frances and Ann came home for the day last week. They are well settled in Bicton House, an' Frances has now been made up to lady's maid. She's a good girl an' sends me as much as she can. They did ask if Mary could join them but I need her at home, Jack." Each snippet of news helped to settle his mind and reinforce his determination to return home by the spring. "William has been good to us since he got back home. I know Susannah gives him a hell of a time if she catches him giving us anything, but he's gettin' plenty of work."

"How's our John doing?"

"He's still working on the fishing boats in Scotland, we don't hear much from him, but no doubt he'll turn up one of these days. Sometimes brothers need to be apart for a bit."

Much to Hannah's surprise Jack did not ask after his mother. During the past three months Anne had barely left the house and now spent most of her time sitting in front of the fire. *It would be enough to unhinge him in his present state*, thought Hannah, and wisely decided to wait for the results of her appeal to Colonel Pinny.

After an hour the couple said a tearful farewell and Hannah left to catch the evening coach. She had plenty of time to construct a heart-rending letter in her mind during the long and uncomfortable ride back to Hangman's Stone. The picture she painted was shocking, and became more so the longer she thought about it. Hannah left no doubt in the recipient's mind that as a result of her husband's unjust incarceration she and her family were suffering severe hardship. The journey seemed endless and it was past midnight when at last the coachman called out, "Hangman's Stone. Passengers for Beer disembark." Hannah was the only passenger travelling to Beer that night and she stepped down onto the road into pitch darkness to make her way down the rocky lane into the village.

Abraham and his two sisters were sitting at the table playing Jack

straws when Hannah reached home. They jumped up with relief at seeing their mother, the roughly fashioned straws scattering over the floor.

"My poor feet," said Hannah, as she wearily sank into a chair. Her daughters were quick to help and pulled off her muddy boots and rubbed her sore toes. Hannah looked at the top of Elizabeth's head and, not for the first time, thought that she would not be long for this world. Her skin was translucent and it was possible to see the delicate blue veins just below the surface.

"Thank you, my dears," said Hannah gratefully. "Now let me tell you news of your father."

Abraham leaned forward and listened to his mother's story. He was wise enough to recognise that his mother was protecting them from the truth. "When's he comin' out, Mother?" he queried.

Hannah paused, and avoiding the question, quickly constructed a positive reply.

"What I'm goin' to do next is write to Colonel Pinny in Lyme an' ask if he can use his influence to get your father early release. He's too old to be stuck in there. It's freezing cold, and the walls is running with damp. Oh Lord," Hannah's hand flew to her mouth, "I forgot to ask, how's Anne?"

Abraham looked downcast.

"Mary's bin' in with her each day an' night, but looks like she's fadin' fast. We asked Reverend Cutliffe to come up an' see her yesterday, see if it would cheer her up, but if anythin' it made her worse."

"Poor old stick," said Hannah sadly. "I'll go over as soon as I've finished this drink."

Chapter 24

After resting for a while Hannah walked next door to her mother-in-law's cottage. A dim light flickered in the window from a small beeswax lamp. Hannah gently pushed the door open to see Mary sitting by her grandmother's bed holding her hand. She looked at her mother anxiously.

"I'm glad you're here, Mother. It's not good. She's hardly opened her eyes since this morning. The only ones she wants is Father an' John. When she does talk she asks me where John is, I don't know what to say to her."

Hannah sat down quietly and took Anne's hand; a strong wrinkled hand, used to hard work, but now lying still. "Hello, Mother. I've just got back from Dorchester, visiting Jack. He said to tell you that he'll be home soon."

Anne stirred at the sound of Hannah's voice, her eyes slowly opened and focused on her daughter-in-law's face. "When?" she said clearly, fixing Hannah with a steady gaze.

"He's hoping it's goin' to be in the next week or so, Mother. It won't do for him to see you like this, so I want you to take some food, and sit up a little."

Hannah warmed some milk and cut up a small amount of bread into it with a generous noggin of brandy. Using a tiny spoon she fed Anne as if she were a small child, gently chiding, tempting and encouraging, until the bowl was empty. Mary watched her mother as she leaned over the old woman, a feeling of deep weariness creeping through her body.

"You get on to bed, Mary. I'll sit up with mother for a while," said Hannah, and stroked her daughter's hair. "You're a good girl, Mary. I don't know what I'd do without you."

Mary looked near to tears. Now thirteen, she was her mother's constant companion but the last year had been hard for both of them.

"Go on to bed, my dear. I'll call you if there's any change."

Hannah put another log on the fire and prepared herself for a long night. She looked around the tiny cottage and remembered the year she had married Jack and moved in with his mother, thirty-one years ago.

"I was just remembering when I married Jack, Mother, and we moved into this cottage with you," she said, not knowing if Anne could hear her or would respond.

Anne opened her eyes briefly and smiled. Encouraged by her response, Hannah plumped up her duck-down pillow and smoothed the coverlet.

"You were as green as grass, girl. Don't think you knew what you'd let yourself in for," Anne whispered. "Never thought you'd make a go of it, but I was wrong."

Hannah sat back in the chair and thought back over the years. Anne had been with her through some of the best and worst times of her life. *Eight children*, thought Hannah, shaking her head. *She was with me through the labour of every one, strong as a rock. Thank you, Mother.* A wave of love and gratitude surged through Hannah, as she thought about the unstinting affection and support this tough, thorny woman had given her. *She's bin closer to me than my own*, she thought.

Hannah could see that it was too tiring for Anne to talk so she dozed for a while. Around 3a.m. Anne stirred. Hannah woke instantly and sat closer to her bed. "Can I get something for you, Mother?"

Anne looked up at Hannah and grasped her hand strongly. "Tell Jack he's bin a good son to me an' I'm sorry."

Hannah could see that Anne would not last the rest of the night and went over to get the children. "It's too late now to get Frances and Ann, but run down an' get William," she said to Abraham.

Anne died just as the dawn light was breaking. Most of her grandchildren were there to say goodbye, but the one person she wanted more than any was Jack. His name was the last word to pass her lips.

Hannah washed Anne's body and made her look tidy and presentable. William had ordered a coffin, and as soon as it

163

arrived Anne would be properly laid out, for people in the village to pay their respects.

"This will be the first time in a long while we've all bin' together, Mother," said William, who was not usually given to sentimentality. "I'm goin' to make sure the old girl has a good send-off. It's all arranged for next Wednesday, so there'll be time for Frances and Ann to get here."

Frances was now married to the Assistant Head Gardener at Bicton House. The couple had a small cottage in the grounds, where they lived with their three-year-old son, William. Ann continued to work in the house as a lady's maid.

Wednesday arrived all too quickly and soon the cottage was full to bursting. The five sisters left the cottage early in the morning and came back to the church with armfuls of laurel branches. It was such a treat for them to be all together, the chatter and the laughter rang around the rafters of the old building.

"Shush," said Frances when Reverend Cutliffe entered through the vestry. The younger girls quickly stifled their mirth and hid behind the pews.

True to his word William provided a good spread at The Dolphin and in Jack's absence took over as head of the household. "I'd like to raise a toast to my grandmother, Anne Newton. She was a hard-working woman and had a heart of gold."

Susannah looked at William with pride. He was now the owner of three boats and looked on with respect around the village, albeit tempered with caution.

By evening Hannah was exhausted and suggested to her daughters that they come back to the cottage. "I can't help but think about your father," she said, when they were all sitting together around the table. "I wrote to the Governor and said Jack's mother had died and could he be given a day out to attend the funeral, but I haven't heard a word in reply."

Frances sniffed. "Well maybe this will teach him a lesson," she said. "Every time he comes out he says it's the last time, but he always slips back into his old ways."

Silence dropped around the table. The younger girls looked at their mother, waiting for her reaction.

"I'll hear none of that from you!" said Hannah, her voice rising sharply. "Without your father we would have had a terrible time of it. You've never had to go without boots on your feet, or somethin' in your belly. An' that's down to your father, so just you remember it. It's working at Bicton House, you're gettin' above yourself."

Frances flushed and muttered an apology. "I'm sorry, Mother, but I've seen the struggles you've had, an' I wish it could have bin' easier for you."

Hannah sighed. "Well, I'm off to bed now, girls. This last week has taken it out of me one way or another. Tomorrow I'm going to write to someone I hope will get your father out of that horrible place."

Hannah was up at first light the next morning, helping Frances dress and feed William, and relishing the small amount of time she had with Ann. All of her busyness was an attempt to avoid the empty feeling of loss and sadness. "Her cottage is going to stand empty till we know what to do with it," said Hannah, looking out across the yard at the small cramped dwelling which held so many memories for all of them. "Come on, Frances, we'll walk up the lane with you," she said, taking William's hand. "That coach is always on time in the morning so you don't want to hang around."

Chapter 25

Sad as she was to see her daughters and grandchild leave, at the forefront of Hannah's mind was achieving Jack's release from gaol. Her letter to the Governor had received no response, so Hannah was unsure whether Jack had been told that his mother had died. When she returned to the house she sat down with pen and paper and wrote the letter, first composed in her mind during the long coach ride back from Dorchester. As she wrote, tears streamed down her face and she felt overwhelmed with grief.

Colonel Pinny,

I would ask that you take pity on our family and help us secure the release of my husband, Mr Jack Rattenbury, who is currently held in Dorchester Gaol.

I have just one son living at home, his name is Abraham and he is sixteen years of age. He is a good hard-working lad and has never been in trouble with the law, but with his father in prison we suffer extreme hardship. Abraham is the family's sole breadwinner. In addition, I have two young daughters, Elizabeth and Ruth, both of whom suffer from ill health. I am greatly concerned for their future without a father at home to support them.

I implore you to consider this matter with the utmost urgency as I am now out of funds and must seek financial help from the parish, a situation of which I am deeply ashamed.

I await your reply with sincere wishes that you can find it in your heart to help us.

Hannah Rattenbury nee Partridge

That evening Hannah explained to Mary and Abraham what she had done, and that she intended to walk to Lyme in the morning to deliver the letter herself. "I need to get some fresh air and blow some of the cobwebs out. I'll be back by four o'clock. Mary, here's a shillin' to get some dabs. Make sure you get a good few, I'll be starvin' by the time I get in."

Hannah left the house before anyone stirred, apart from Abraham that is, who was off on one of William's fishing boats, well before dawn. She walked down Fore Street and up onto the cliff path. Stretching before her was Lyme Bay, the coastline delicately wreathed in the early morning mist and curving out to Portland Bill. *This feels good,* she thought. *I need to get out of the village and give my brain a rest.* A smile spread across Hannah's face. *A whole day of freedom, when I can listen to the birds on the Undercliff, and take my time.*

Much as she enjoyed the walk Hannah was weary by the time she reached Silver Street and knocked on Colonel Pinny's red-painted front door. A plump maid answered her firm bang of the knocker and left Hannah on the pavement while she delivered the letter.

"Come in, come in, my dear," a voice boomed from the hall and Hannah looked up to see the familiar face of an elderly gentleman with a shock of white hair. He stood in the doorway of his fine oak-panelled study.

"It's a very long time since we last met, Mrs Rattenbury. Your father was a regular visitor here. Can I offer you a cup of tea?"

The maid hovered in the background and quickly left for the kitchen when Hannah accepted the offer of refreshment.

"I decided to deliver this letter by hand, sir, as my request has become a matter of some urgency."

Colonel Pinny read the letter, shaking his head. He had great sympathy for Hannah's plight, and was somewhat mystified as to how a woman from such a respectable family could have married a man like Jack Rattenbury.

He put the letter carefully down on his desk and turned to Hannah, his face showing every sign of compassion and concern. "I think your family deserves my support, Mrs Rattenbury," he said. "Your father was a great help to me as a young man."

Hannah smiled, a cautious tremulous smile which brought her near to tears. "I have thought long and hard before approaching you, Colonel Pinny but as I have explained in the letter, we are in desperate straits, and Jack's health will undoubtedly suffer if he stays longer in that terrible place."

"Please leave this matter with me, Mrs Rattenbury. I have such fond memories of your dear father and mother and will do my utmost to help you. I must implore you, however, to persuade your husband to take a different course in life – one in which he earns his living within the law."

Hannah gave the Colonel her assurance that she would set out to divert Jack from smuggling, and once again thanked him for his kind consideration.

After lunch Colonel Pinny wrote a letter to the Governor of Dorchester prison, in which he stressed his connection with Hannah's father, and his conviction that Hannah would exert her influence on Jack that he return to a law-abiding life. On receiving the missive the following morning the Governor read it disbelievingly; bellows of cynical laughter echoed around his office. "Josh," he shouted for the gaoler. You can tell Rattenbury that he'll be released on Friday, after the hearing, an' I don't want to see sight of his miserable face here again."

Prior to his release Jack received a short message from Colonel Pinny suggesting that, should he be granted early release, he would in future diligently provide for his family within the law. He also recommended that Jack join Beer Parish Church where he would receive spiritual sustenance from Reverend Cutliffe. The latter piece of advice brought a smile to Jack's face. He had provided the Reverend with a few kegs on many occasions to keep him sweet, while hiding smuggled goods in a cave behind the church.

Chapter 26

Following this last conviction, William had been released after six months, while Jack languished in Dorchester gaol for a further eighteen months. During this time William had acquired three boats with the help of Abe Mutter, and greatly aided by the avaricious determination of his wife.

William had established a reputation, up and down the coast, as someone who would stop at nothing to pull off a successful run of contraband. He considered himself above the law and what happened to Albert Rankin was evidence of this.

After his release from Dorchester, William had watched, waited and questioned anyone who could help him track down the person who had informed the revenue men about that last ill-fated trip he had made to Cherbourg with his father. This search had become an obsession and shortly before Jack's release, William uncovered the evidence which proved beyond doubt that Albert Rankin was the culprit. Nothing would now get in the way of William exacting his revenge. Albert, who was by now in his late fifties, was found one morning, tied hand and foot, on the top of Beer Head. He had received a severe beating, which had left him close to death. It was generally known in the village that William had administered the punishment but none would have dared speak of it openly.

Jack walked towards the prison gates; a feeling of elation made his heart pound against his ribs. He wasted no time on reflection, even when confronted with the inert body of a young man, swinging from the gibbet. *I can't wait to get back home and see Hannah*, this thought dominated his mind as he strode down the long drive, wanting to put as much distance as possible between himself and that hateful place.

The landlord of The Crown was just opening up when Jack reached the inn.

"What time is the next coach for Lyme, sir?" asked Jack.

Jack's pallor was not alluded to but the landlord had seen it before and recognised a man who had not seen sunlight for a good while. "You've got a two-hour wait, sir, but if you have the price I can give you a good breakfast and a jar of our best ale."

Jack needed no encouragement. The very thought of sitting down to a plate of thick fat bacon was enough to make his mouth water. William had made sure his father had received his fare back to Beer and had generously included an extra guinea. The money sat reassuringly in Jack's pocket.

"I can think of no better way to spend the next two hours, sir. Please pile the plate high and I'll certainly do it justice."

Jack sat back in a comfortable chair by the fire and savoured the indescribably sweet taste of freedom. After the grim grey walls of a prison cell the muted colours of the inn appeared to leap and dance before him. He stroked the worn, faded armchair, which had seen better days, and wanted to laugh out loud with the pleasure of it. The landlord brought through a sizzling plate of bacon, piled high as Jack had requested.

"Enjoy your meal, sir. I expect it's a long while since you've seen one like it."

The coach arrived on time, heralding its arrival with a long blast on the horn. Jack took the seat behind the coachman. The morning was clear, and as it had been dry for some while, the road was in a fair condition. They made good time, although Jack had time to reflect again on the considerable discomfort endured when travelling by coach. When the horses at last pulled into Lyme Jack had had enough of the swaying and constant crash of the tortured wheels.

"I think I'll leave you here, sir," he said to the coachman, having decided to walk the last part of his journey along the coastal path to Seaton. Jack felt weak and stiff. He was aware that the months he had spent in gaol had taxed him, both mentally and physically. *I need some time to think things over before I get back home*, he thought. *It's nearly two years since I've been in Beer, a lot must have changed in that time.*

Within a short while Jack was out of town and on a small track leading to the wooded coastal path. The fresh salty smell of the sea soon swept away his melancholy ruminations and rid him of the stench of Dorchester Gaol. By evening he had reached the cliffs above the village and made straight for home. As he walked up the Causeway he could see a curl of smoke drifting up from the cottage chimney and chuckled to himself. *Just two more minutes and I'll have my boots off and be sitting in front of my own fire*, he thought.

The door was on the latch and before he could get across the step he was surrounded by his three girls, Mary, Elizabeth and Ruth. Abe and Hannah were on their feet in an instant and the all-embracing warmth of his family's welcome drew Jack in and brought a lump to his throat.

"By God, it's wonderful to see you all," he said, throwing his arms wide and drinking in their smiling faces. When the initial excitement of their father's arrival was over, Elizabeth and Ruth slipped into the background. They were old enough to remember Jack but felt shy around this unfamiliar figure. Far from shy, Mary smothered her father with affection, rushing around to get his food and a mug of ale, while Hannah sat and beamed with joyful relief. The evening drew on and the girls went up to bed, leaving Jack, Abraham and Hannah sitting in front of the fire.

"I'm afraid we've got some bad news for you, Father," said Abraham.

Hannah's eyes darted to Jack's face and she recoiled, not wanting to witness his distress on hearing of his mother's death.

Jack looked at his youngest son and said without prompting, "It's mother, she's dead."

Abraham nodded, "How did you know?"

"All the way home I've known that somethin' was different," said Jack. "When I walked past her window an' there was no light, I was sure of it."

Abraham told his father every detail of Anne's last illness and how she had died peacefully in her bed. "Your name was the last word on her lips, Father. You an' our John. She kept on asking where you both were."

Jack's face sank into a mask of sadness. His shoulders slumped and he stared into the fire, as if hoping his mother's face would materialise from the flames.

"She had a good funeral; our William saw to that," said Hannah, reaching out for his hand. "Her gravestone is being made up the quarry. It should be in place by next month. But we wanted you home to say what words you wanted on it."

"Think I'll go up now," Jack said. The news had drained him and a heavy weariness settled uncomfortably around his heart. "I couldn't have wished for a better mother," he muttered. "She stood firm by me through the worst of it".

Walking down onto the beach with William the following day, Jack was aware of a subtle change. Men called out to him as they always had, curious to know how he was making out, but it soon became clear that William had stepped firmly into his father's boots during the time he had been away. Jack looked over the vessels his eldest son had purchased with the help of Abe Mutter and an undisclosed party.

"What do you think, Father?"

"Good strong luggers by the looks of 'em, son. Three boats, not bad, eh?"

William looked at his father closely and for the first time saw that he was growing old. This last stint in prison had taken something indefinable out of him, and Anne's death had added to his loss of vigour. "You're looking a bit grey around the gills, Father. Could do with a bit of fresh air and mother's cookin'." William rested his arm across Jack's shoulders and was conscious of his frailty. "Let's go up to The Dolphin, I've got a few things to talk over with you."

Father and son walked up Sea Hill and Jack could scarcely not notice the respect with which William was received. He felt proud, but was also aware of a slight wariness in relation to his son.

The landlord greeted Jack with affection. "Back again, Jack! You don't look as if your little holiday has done you much good. Here, have a drink on the house," he said, handing Jack a foaming jar of ale.

William and Jack took their seats by the fire. The tap room in The Dolphin was as familiar to Jack as his own kitchen. He looked around at the walls, stained with tobacco and listened to the talk of men who had just spent hours at sea and were enjoying a drink before returning to mend nets and prepare bait. William leant forward, keeping his voice low.

"Things have moved on since you went inside, Father. The Coastguard, as the bastards are now known, get onto every move we make, they watch us day and night. They're offering good money for information, so there's more spies in the village. It's hard to know who you can trust, so I keep the contacts to people we know. Abe has been a big help, an' somebody he told me to make contact with in France, your old mate Louis Claude. What I'm leading up to is this, I've a big run goin' on Friday night, a very big run. Our three boats is goin' over to Cherbourg on the evening tide to pick up a load of kegs and we intend landing the lot back here on the beach by 1a.m. Sunday. We'll be taking a risk but I've got about a hundred carriers and ten batmen, so we should get it in quickly and off through the lanes in no time."

Jack sat back in his chair and stared at his son in amazement. "Bloody hell, William! That's goin' to take some doin'."

William threw back his head and laughed. "Well, I'm gambling that the idea of landing straight onto the beach is so damned cheeky that no one would believe we'd try it. They'll be looking everywhere but Beer. We've already set off a few false rumours about a big run coming in just off Sidmouth."

"I'm up for a trip over the water, William," said Jack gamely, but could see immediately that William was not at all keen on the idea.

"Not this time, Father," he said, shaking his head firmly. "It's goin' to be rough if we get spotted, and the last thing you need is to end up back inside." He stood up abruptly, "Do as I say and stay indoors."

Jack was taken aback by William's harsh and unequivocal rejection. He rubbed his knees and downed his ale quickly. "Good luck, son. No doubt I'll hear how it's gone before long."

William walked back down to his cottage and was met by Susannah. She stood by the back door, her hands spread on her broad hips. "Still running round after your father, I see. What's he ever done for you, that's what I'd like to know."

William looked at his wife with barely concealed distaste and thought, not for the first time, that he had jumped too quickly when she had suggested they marry.

"Have you ever thought, woman, that there's one hell of a lot you don't know? Get out of my sight!" William gave Susannah a shove that sent her stumbling backwards.

"Bloody idiot, a pox on you!" she shouted, and ducked as William raised his fist.

The children, who until that point had been hanging onto her skirts, ran for the beach. Seeing that this time she had gone too far, Susannah quickly got to her feet and attempted a smile. Softening her voice, she said, "What time are you off?"

William looked up and noted the change, but remained cautious. "We're leaving on the evening tide and if all goes to plan we should be coming back into Beer Roads around 1a.m. Sunday."

"I'll be keeping watch with a few others along Beer Head. The bloody Coastguard are gettin' to know every hiding place up there, but me and Anna Gush have found a good place, just below the cliff edge."

"Well, I'm going to bed for a kip before I go," said William. "How about coming up?"

Chapter 27

The three luggers, carefully disguised as a fishing trip, set out as planned on the evening tide. The wind was set fair, north to north-west. They expected no problems on the way over to the Cherbourg peninsula and they encountered none. William was able to sit and think through the days ahead, yet again, although it was too late now to change anything. His mind wandered over the detailed plan, worked out in The Dolphin with Abe Mutter. It was Abe who had first suggested that he get in touch with Louis Claude, after a succession of unsuccessful runs with unreliable agents. "He's been a good mate to your father over the years," said Abe, "an' I'm sure he'd help us out. The next time you're in Cap la Hague, William, look him up."

After several months of enquiries William had come across Louis sitting in a small restaurant in Omonville enjoying a good fish meal and a fine bottle of Burgundy. He sat down and introduced himself. "Bonjour, Monsieur Claude, I am Jack Rattenbury's son. No doubt you remember my father?"

"Yes, yes, William, of course I remember," said the Frenchman, rising to his feet and giving William a slight bow. The men shook hands warmly. "Please join me."

William needed no further encouragement and ordered some food and another bottle of wine. Several hours passed while they talked business and politics. Louis listened sympathetically to William's aggravation concerning the constant harassment he suffered from Coastguards. "They make my life a bloody misery. It's one law for them an' one for us. If they gets the chance of a couple of kegs they don't turn it down, you mark my words. My father's spent the last two years in gaol on a trumped-up charge and on the scanty evidence of a piece of rope. It wouldn't have stood up in

Court a few years back, but now they can lock you up for next to nothin'."

Louis expressed his regret on hearing of Jack's time in Dorchester Gaol. "It's time he gave up this risky business, William. You are lucky to catch me, you know. I give myself just six more months and then I am off to the south to rest my bones. In fact, after the war I stayed away from dealing in contraband for a good few years and tried my hand at farming, but I'm not cut out for it."

Louis observed William closely. He could see Jack in him but could also see that William had a tense, driven quality. "Don't take too many chances, William. Life is too short to spend it behind bars, as your father and I well know."

William nodded, not wanting to engage in reminiscing about his father's career, particularly as he could see that the Frenchman was hooked, for one last deal. The run had taken nearly three months to organise and Louis had needed some persuading that it could be carried off at all, but now all the arrangements were in place.

William stood up, and bracing himself against the pitch and roll of the boat, stretched his stiff back. He stared into the darkness, every nerve on edge. *If I can pull this off*, he thought, *I'll be well set up*, and once again went over the figures in his head.

The boats reached Racine beach on Cap la Hague at 10a.m. on Saturday. The morning was bright and clear. William could see Louis standing on the beach, having been forewarned of their arrival by children, who had watched the luggers from the cliffs for the past two hours. William waved and smiled in amusement, watching their small grimy hands stretching out for payment.

The luggers edged as near in as possible to the shallow sandy beach and when they were as close in as they could get, dozens of carriers set out in small boats weighed down with kegs. William watched and counted as the men handed up the spirits from the small tenders bobbing around in the surf. It took three hours to load the three boats and when the job was near completion William went ashore to finalise the contract. He handed over a thick wodge of notes to Louis.

"Many thanks for your help, Monsieur Claude. I doubt we will meet again but I will convey your regards to my father, and I wish you well in your retirement."

Louis stood on the beach watching the ochre sails of the luggers fill, pulling the laden boats towards the open sea. *I've known Jack for forty years,* he thought, *and now, here is his son, in the same risky business.* He shrugged his shoulders, as if needing to shake off any responsibility for the danger William now faced.

The three boats had left Cap la Hague by mid-afternoon and enjoyed a brisk south-east wind. By evening the sky was overcast, with no moon. William listened intently for any sound which would indicate an excise cutter in the area, and had instructed the crews to remain silent throughout the run. He had planned with the two other skippers to head west should they need to escape the Coastguard. He knew the coast between Lyme and Falmouth like the backbone of a mackerel and had located several hidden coves they could slip into should it become necessary. He felt tense and anxious. A large sum was invested in this run. These melancholy thoughts were stifled as he concentrated on keeping the sails trimmed and the lugger pulling strongly through the water.

The shoreline and Seaton Cliffs stood in total darkness as the boats entered Beer Roads, but anyone who knew the beach well could see that the rocks appeared to be further away from the foot of the cliffs, and carts stood in unusual places. No one could be seen but the cove held an air of potent menace. As the three luggers turned into the cove, scores of eyes watched and waited, a hundred bodies crouched, ready to spring.

As William neared the shore he hung over the gunnels and brought the lugger in broadside, followed shortly by the two other skippers. On hearing the stempost hit the shingle, men sprang from the shadows and, running across the beach, formed a chain. They worked soundlessly, in water up to their chests. Fear moved like a whip through their bodies, running with sweat.

At last William's lugger was empty of kegs and he pushed the boat off shore.

The laden carriers moved towards the back of the beach ready to start the journey inland. "This place is givin' me the creeps," muttered one, a short stocky character. His clothes hung on his body in rags, and his face had the drawn, haunted look of a man in need of a night's sleep and a good meal.

The carrier's fears were not unfounded – the beach was under surveillance. Concealed at the top of Seaton Cliffs was a figure standing in the shadows. Shaking with fatigue and hunger, the man watched the scene below, not daring to move. The Coastguard patrol had set off westwards towards Sidmouth, intent on investigating a rumour, circulating around the village, of a big landing due in off Weston Beach. But after several hours of fruitless searching, the weary troop had made their way back towards Beer empty-handed. Earlier in the day, suspicious that no other warnings of a run had been received, a guard had been placed at the top of Seaton Cliffs, well concealed in dense undergrowth. Hours had passed while he studied the horizon as the evening light faded and darkness closed around him. He had not heard the beach fill with carriers, who had slipped through the darkness and clung to the bottom of the cliffs. But something of the tension had risen through the trees and every now and then the stamp of a mule or a muffled cough would send a shiver of apprehension through the guard's exhausted body. And then he heard a sound that could not be muffled – the rasp of a laden lugger hitting the shore, shortly followed by two more.

The guard inched towards the edge of the cliff, and in the gloom could see the shoreline. Three luggers stood broadside, each being unloaded by chains of men handing kegs over their heads onto the waiting carts. Armed batmen stood at intervals watching the cliffs, while one faced out to sea.

The guard felt a cold rivulet of sweat run down his back and knew, without doubt, that should he be spotted the batmen would have no hesitation in hunting him down. He squinted through his spyglass towards the coastal path, just visible on the other side of Beer cove and to his relief he could see a line of men, dressed in the uniform of the

Coastguard, making their way down towards the village. *I'll wait until they get to Common Lane,* thought the guard, desperately trying to keep a grasp on his senses and not panic. At last, the first man appeared on the lane and the guard forced himself to squeeze the trigger of his musket. The roar of the ignited gunpowder rolled around the cliffs and dropped into the throng of men on the beach like a meteor strike. The batmen turned and ran towards Sea Hill, ready to defend the cargo, and as they reached Charlie's Yard a troop of armed Coastguards raced down the hill, led by Lieutenant Bate, shouting orders and firing his pistol in the air.

This is my chance, Bate thought. *I'll bring the Beer smugglers to their knees if it's the last thing I do.*

A contemptuous roar erupted from the carriers as they turned to defend themselves. "Bastards!" they screamed as one, determined not to be taken. Most carried swingle bats, or any weapon which came to hand, and they charged into the body of the Coastguard, driven by fear and an overwhelming rage that they were going to be denied any reward for this long and gruelling night's work.

William leapt into a tender and rowed ashore. By now the beach was filled with men, all engaged in a desperate battle for survival. He threw himself into the scrum and, holding an oar as if it were matchwood, lashed out at the young lieutenant who was wielding a cutlass. The blow caught him off balance and he fell clumsily onto the pebbles. "I'll kill you, you bugger," William yelled, his face contorted into a mask of hatred. He was beside himself with fury and set about the young officer, kicking and beating him with every intention of murder.

Lieutenant Bate was saved from William's murderous assault by a young recruit, Thomas Budden, who had fired his musket directly at William, narrowly missing his head. The officer now stood facing the smugglers, bloodied and injured, but far from beaten. "I'll give the order to shoot the first man to make a move," he shouted, his voice breaking in an effort to rise above the melee.

Many of the carriers, seeing that they were overpowered, had dumped the kegs and melted away into the night. Soon the beach was silent and empty. "Collect up the tubs, men," ordered Lieutenant Bate. "A cutter will be coming in shortly to pick up the prisoners. I want a strict inventory taken of all the tubs and flagons found on this beach." *No doubt I'll get a commendation for this night's work,* he thought.

Five men were arrested that night and the Courts meted out severe punishments, giving the irrevocable message that smuggling, on the scale carried out over the past hundred years, would have to stop.

When the men were rounded up, William was nowhere to be found. The shot whistling past his head had shaken him to his senses and, looking wildly around the beach, he could see that it had become a rout. He found one of his skippers hiding under the cliffs and silently the two men slipped away.

Chapter 28

Elizabeth and Ruth sat in the window of the cottage; both had plump lace pillows sitting comfortably on their knees. It was early evening and soon the sun would drop behind the hill on the opposite side of the valley, drawing the Causeway into the dark still night. Elizabeth looked up and smiled at her mother who was stirring a pot of broth. "We'll need to light a candle soon, Mother."

Hannah moved over to her daughters and watched their thin white fingers flying over the bobbins, marvelling at the delicate lacework emerging from the pins etched into a design on the pillow. *I'm so thankful they have mastered a skill which will earn some money and keep them employed,* she thought.

Both girls were in poor health. Elizabeth had suffered from a weak heart from birth. This condition had severely stunted her growth and she was often breathless and unable to walk across the kitchen without support. She had just passed her thirteenth birthday and spent her time making lace and helping her mother with light tasks in the kitchen and garden.

Ruth had suffered a bout of pneumonia at six months old. The illness had left her with severely damaged lungs and now, at seven years of age, she also was constrained by physical weakness. A placid artless child, she would sit for many hours patiently working on a simple collar, happy to listen to her mother and Mary chattering while they cleaned the cottage and brought in wood for the fire.

The sisters were very close and spent all day and every day in each other's company, gently teasing each other and enjoying an amiable competition as to who could produce the finest and most unusual designs. Elizabeth always won, of course, but was careful not to discourage Ruth. Lace-edged handkerchiefs, collars, falls for bonnets and cobweb scarves,

181

all were finished to perfection for people who could afford to buy. Hannah sold their fine work to a local dealer and was well known for her ability to drive a hard bargain. Even so the payment she received was a pittance in relation to the hours of labour needed to produce such superb workmanship.

Mary looked around the cottage and thought back on how much the family had changed during the past three years. She remained at home helping Hannah and resisting any pressure to go into service as her sisters Frances and Ann had done.

"I'd rather stay in the village," Mary replied, when her mother, concerned that her daughter was not broadening her horizons, would chide Mary and suggest she apply for work at Shute House or Bicton. Secretly Hannah was relieved that Mary wanted to stay in the village. Life had not been easy for her while Jack was in Dorchester Gaol and the responsibility of caring for Elizabeth and Ruth on her own would have been daunting indeed.

"Well, no doubt you'll pick up with a nice boy sooner or later, Mary. There's plenty to choose from in the village."

Mary looked irritated at this suggestion and vowed to herself that she would avoid this fate if at all possible. "Grandmother did very well on her own, an' that's how I want to be. She didn't need any man to look after her."

At this Hannah would shake her head and purse her lips. "We'll see about that, young lady. Life was never easy for your grandmother and what she would have done in her later years without us, I don't know."

Jack was now the only male living in the household. He was fussed over and had his every need catered for by a covey of women, all wanting to keep him home and safe. This situation was entirely to Jack's liking, and there was nothing he enjoyed more than to sit before the fire of an evening, surrounded by his family, and talk about his adventures. No doubt if the sons had been present the competition to out-talk or outdo the others would have ensured that the tales degenerated into a fierce competition. But as things were, Jack enjoyed a rapt and adoring audience.

Spring had brought a welcome rise in the temperature along the coast, giving Jack an ideal time to adjust to life outside prison. He spent his days fishing and working for Abe Mutter. The two friends often sat on Ponds Wall above the beach, talking about the last calamitous run. Jack commiserated endlessly over Abe's substantial financial loss.

"I threw away a good wedge of money that night, Jack. The only good thing to come out of it was that the luggers didn't get taken by the Excise. Why they didn't, I don't know. I think they must have bin' so overjoyed at collecting the complete haul of kegs that they decided to be generous for once."

Jack could only listen and wonder in this discussion. He had been amazed that an experienced free trader like Abe would have agreed to land three luggers, fully laden with contraband, on Beer beach, practically under the noses of the Coastguard. *Our William must have got him all fired up*, he would think, as Abe rambled on, and felt thankful that no one, apart from a few carriers, had been arrested on that awful night.

"But that skipper your William took off with must still have the third lugger. I never worked out who he was in all the mayhem, but no sightings have bin' made of it, so I expect he sold it off quick before the Excise caught up."

Jack had no answers to any of these questions. He had done as William had told him, stayed at home and kept out of it. For most of the villagers this seemed out of character for Jack, and most believed that he knew far more than he let on. "Seen anythin' of William lately?" He was asked this question many times while working around the beach, but Jack always kept his replies light and uninformative. "Last I heard he was working on a fishin' smack down round Falmouth, doin' well, I believe."

This reply was entirely a figment of Jack's imagination. Susannah had hinted that William may be in Scotland, working with John, but she had no evidence of this. Her life had changed since William's disappearance and she spent her days working in The Dolphin and trying to control her three sons who had gone wild since their father had left home. "Get down on that beach and earn a few coppers," she would scream, when life in the cottage became unbearable. And on receiving a good cuff around his ear, the eldest son, Jake, now fourteen years of age, would leave the house and sometimes not be seen for weeks.

Susannah rarely came to visit Hannah. The two women would see one another at the brook when collecting water, or down on the beach where Hannah sold fish, but feelings between them were always strained, and there was little common ground. But, on a low day, when Hannah had spent hours brooding on the lack of news from William and John, she would stop and make an effort to talk to her daughter-in-law. "Any news, Susannah?" And no matter how she tried, her voice always sounded stiff and aloof. Susannah's head would jerk up, her mouth held in a hard line, and if at all possible she would avoid Hannah's sad eyes. "Not a bloody word from the man!" she'd say bitterly. Many more angry and frustrated words would bubble into her mouth, but Susannah knew that Hannah would never give her the satisfaction of fighting back, and so the two women would part, and continue on their way.

One evening, on returning home after a long day working on the beach, Hannah was met by Mary running down the road holding a letter. Hannah's heart leapt and she struggled to stifle her initial disappointment when finding that it was not from William or John as she had hoped, but from Frances and Ann. They were travelling over to Beer the following week to visit the family. On reaching home Hannah soon put aside her yearning to see her sons, and looked forward with enthusiasm to seeing her eldest daughters again. The cottage received a special clean. Elizabeth and Ruth were put to peeling vegetables and keeping a watch on the lane when the day arrived.

"Here they be," called Elizabeth, who had been sitting at the window all morning. She walked out to the gate and waved her handkerchief at her sisters. William, Frances's eldest child, ran ahead, barely containing his excitement at the thought of meeting his relations. He knew that all sorts of treats would be waiting and, for one day at least, he would be pampered.

Frances walked slowly, carrying her second child in a shawl. Life had been kind to her at Bicton House. She had worked her way up to Housekeeper and was highly thought of by her employers. When she married the Assistant Head Gardener and moved into a small cottage in the grounds, Hannah had been delighted, and proud that her eldest daughter had done so well. Now comfortably settled into matrimony and motherhood, Frances still retained that strong assurance of her own rightness in most situations.

Ann had never married. This situation had been of prurient interest to Frances, who in years past had persistently questioned Ann about her single status. "Let it be. Married life is just not for me, leave it at that," Ann would snap at her sister. But this explanation had never quite satisfied Frances and she continued to probe and tease, much to her sister's annoyance.

What would have fascinated Frances even more was the fact that Ann had been engaged in a long and ongoing affair with the cousin of Lord Rolle. Ann was just sixteen years old on their first meeting and the attraction on both sides was instantaneous. Ann would never have been able to explain the attraction she had felt for a man who was certainly old enough to be her father. It was a secret and wonderful part of her life, but one that had ensnared her. No boy of her own age ever measured up in Ann's mind to this kind and charming man, and she lived her life in endless waiting for their short precious times together.

Soon after Frances and Ann arrived, Jack came up from the beach, followed soon after by Abraham and his wife Clara. The cottage was full to overflowing. Jack and Hannah sat looking proudly at this near-complete family gathering.

Frances looked closely at her mother, questions hovering around her lips. "Any news of William?" she asked.

"Well, strangely enough, Frances, I did hear a rumour from Susannah last week that William had been spotted in Scotland working with John on the salmon boats, delivering between Banff and Aberdeen. She was told by a man Abe

Mutter had met in Lyme. It's quite possible that it's true, as there's a lot of Devon men workin' in Scotland on the boats."

"And how is Susannah?"

Hannah looked pensive and replied with caution. "I can't say that I know, Frances. We see one another in the lane and when collecting water, but we've never bin' close, as you know. I think she has had some problems in regard to the last run. People have spoken out against her. She was keeping watch on the cliffs with Anna Gush that night when the excise men walked right past their hiding place below the cliffs, on their way back down to the beach, but no fire was set to give William a warning. Some say they were drunk on cider. All I know is that since William's bin gone her boys have run wild. I've told her that you'll be here tonight, and she may look in after she has finished work at The Dolphin."

Frances listened to her mother. She was talking of another life, one that had been part of her childhood, but now seemed alien and dark. "How about Father? Is he keeping away from trading these days?"

Hannah smiled and smoothed down her apron. "For once in my married life, Frances, I think I can answer you honestly. Your father is slowing down. I know that sounds sad, but I've not seen him as happy and content as he is now for years. He gets work from Abe and no doubt he is tempted to take on a run at times, but to my knowledge he has stayed clear of it since coming out of Dorchester. But now you can give me some news. What's happening with our Ann? She shows no interest in getting married, and trying to get her to talk about her life at Bicton is like prizing a limpet off a rock."

Frances laughed. The baby, sitting quietly on her lap, started to cry and Frances wiped her face clean and settled her down for a sleep. "I have tried to get it out of her, Mother, and all I can say is that a rumour went around the house early last year that she was in love with the cousin of Lord Rolle. I watched her for a time, an' it did seem to be that she was away visiting when I know he was in the area. I did ask her outright one day, but she near on bit my head off, an' told me not to be so stupid. She seems happy enough, but other than me she don't have many friends in the house."

Hannah was amazed and shocked at this disclosure. Her shoulders twitched in disapproval. "All I can say, Frances, is that his sort only wants our kind for one thing, an' when their interest wanes you be left, mark my words. But surely our Ann has more sense than that?"

The two-day visit came to an end, and sadly, Frances and Ann packed up to leave. "I'll walk up to the cross with you," said Jack, and placed William on his shoulders, now padded out with muscle, and strong once again from his work on the beach.

The months passed into a year and it was becoming apparent that Elizabeth was failing. Her heart often felt swollen and sore in her chest and most days she was unable to get out of her chair. "What is to be done, Jack? I can't bear to lose her," Hannah would whisper late at night. But Jack had no answer. "We can call in the doctor if you like Hannah, but he always says there's nothin' he can do. That stuff he gave her last time made it all worse, as far as I could see."

Hannah listened sadly. She knew this to be true and searched to find a way of accepting that Elizabeth had little time left. Night after night she sat by her bed and gently wiped her brow with cool water from the brook. Elizabeth would look kindly at her mother, her soft brown eyes full of sympathy for the pain Hannah was suffering. "I'm not frightened, Mother," she said softly one night, and before Hannah could reply, she had slipped away.

Hannah was surprised to find that she accepted her daughter's death without overwhelming grief. There was no weeping and wailing and the family gathered together to give her a loving funeral before she was buried. But for Ruth the loss was devastating. She mourned Elizabeth and spent days sitting in the window, unable to touch her lace-making and keening for her sister.

"I'm going to get you out of the house for a while, Ruth. How about I get Abe to give you a lift down to the beach on his cart?"

For the first time in weeks Ruth smiled and clapped her hands. "I haven't bin down there for nearly two years," she said, and took a brush to her hair and pinned it up on top of her head.

Hannah was delighted with her response and asked Jack to pass on the message to Abe. "You can tell him to clean that cart out. We don't want to get down there looking filthy."

Ruth waited impatiently the next day, and soon after noon she could hear the cart's wheels rumbling up the lane. Abe had given his old cart a good sweep out and even tied a ribbon on the mare's bridle to make her look smart. "Climb in, Hannah, I'll lift the little princess up for you," he said jovially.

Hannah wrapped her daughter in a blanket and they set off down through the village. Ruth's young face was a picture of pure delight. Hannah's hair was now thin and white but she had taken care to pile it on top of her head, held in place by a yellow straw bonnet.

"Here we are, Miss," said Abe, and gently lifted Ruth down onto the cobbles at the top of Sea Hill. "I'll come back for you in an hour."

Mother and daughter sat on Pond's Wall looking out to sea and let the bustling swirl of the beach lift their spirits. On the shore they could see Jack washing out a boat after a morning's fishing. Gulls screamed over his head, searching for scraps.

Hannah watched him work, a gentle smile playing around her lips, and she remembered that first morning on Lyme quay. *What a dance I've been on,* she thought, *but I wouldn't have missed a day of it.*

GLOSSARY

Boarding blunderbuss	Small firearm
Creeping	Method used by the excise men to locate submerged tubs, with pronged hooks
Crop-sowing	Sinking a raft of tubs in a marked position offshore
Cutter	A single-masted vessel, rigged like a sloop but with a running bowsprit
Dragoon	Mounted soldier
Excise man	An officer responsible for assessing and collecting excise duty
Free trader	A smuggler
Lugger	A vessel with four-cornered sails, rigged fore-and-aft
Privateer	A privately owned, armed vessel holding a government commission to wage war on enemy ships
Riding Officer	Officer in the Customs Service appointed to patrol on horseback
Run	Contraband operation
Spout lantern	A signalling lantern designed to send out a beam of light through a long spout
Swingle bat	Long wooden stave
Tub	A wooden cask holding a half-anker of spirits (approximately four gallons)

REFERENCE BOOKS

Smuggler   Eileen Hathaway
Jack Rattenbury and his adventures in
Devon, Dorset and Cornwall 1778-1844

Smuggling in Devon and Cornwall   Mary Waugh
1700-1850
Countryside Books, 1991

A Short History of the English People   John Richard Green
Macmillan, 1911

Smuggling Days and Smuggling Ways   Lt. Henry N. Shore RN
Cassell, 1892

Beer in Time and Tide   Arthur J. Chapple, 1986

Beer in Smuggling Times   Arthur J. Chapple, 1989

Memoirs of a Smuggler   Jack Rattenbury
J. Harvey, Sidmouth, 1837

Honest Thieves   F.F. Nichols
William Heineman Ltd

Historical Overview of Devon   David Nash Ford

Devon Building   Peter Beacham
Devon Books, 1990

Devon Thatch   Jo Cox and John Thorpe
Devon Books

Devon Notes and Queries   West Country Studies
Vol. IV, pp.257–260   Library - Exeter Flying Post